# Windy John's Rainbow and The Pot o' Gold

*And More Great Stories*

Joyce Rapier

PUBLISH AMERICA

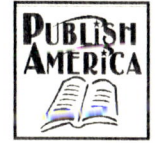

PublishAmerica
Baltimore

© 2003 by Joyce Rapier.

All rights reserved. No part of this book may be reproduced, stored in a retrieval system or transmitted in any form or by any means without the prior written permission of the publishers, except by a reviewer who may quote brief passages in a review to be printed in a newspaper, magazine or journal.

First printing

ISBN: 1-4137-0248-1
PUBLISHED BY PUBLISHAMERICA BOOK PUBLISHERS
www.publishamerica.com
Baltimore

Printed in the United States of America

# ACKNOWLEDGEMENT

To my father, J.D. Brannam, better known as Windy John, whose love for spinning yarns is the depth and backbone of this book. Here's to you, Windy John! I hope you enjoy looking down from heaven, watching with great pride as we laugh at your stories and reflect back on the memories of your childhood and draw upon our own quiet moments.

# IN DEDICATION

In memory to my father, Windy John,
With love, your daughter.

With great appreciation to PublishAmerica, Inc., who made my lifelong dream of being a published author come true.

To my husband, Dan, for understanding my idiosyncratic tendencies.

To all of my readers: Thank you very much.

# HILL TALK WORD GUIDE

| | |
|---|---|
| Abidin': | Putting up with something / keep in mind |
| Afore: | Just before doing something |
| Agin: | Try that one more time |
| Aiggs: | Eggs / chicken / duck / |
| Ain't: | Not going to do something |
| Airy: | Nothing / light and breezy |
| Allus: | Always |
| Ary: | Nothing / nil / zilch / zero |
| | |
| Beeswax: | None of your business |
| Best be: | Getting on about intended business |
| Betwixt: | Between |
| Blak Salve: | Stinking black rubbing compound for skin |
| Blud: | Blood |
| 'Bout: | Almost / nearly |
| Brew Woods: | Hiding place for moonshine whiskey |
| Brung: | Brought |
| | |
| Cain't: | Unable to do something / unwilling to try |
| Chiggers: | Little red burrowing bugs causing skin irritation / itch |
| Coal Oil: | Kerosene / fuel for burning / skin healer for wounds |
| Coupl'a: | Two |
| Crawlt: | Crawl / crawled |
| Daith: | Death / final |

| | |
|---|---|
| Dawgs: | Dogs / critters |
| Don't'cha': | Don't you do whatever you have a mind to do |
| Daren't: | Scared of / shouldn't |
| Dassant: | Better not do |
| | |
| Er: | Are |
| Et: | Ate |
| Et'em: | Finished eating |
| | |
| Feered: | Afraid |
| Fer: | For |
| Fetch: | Gather / collect |
| Figger: | Ponder / think |
| Fixin': | Starting to do a task / thinking of beginning to do |
| Flung: | Threw an object |
| Frum: | From |
| | |
| Gaumin: | Messing into other people's business / mess making |
| Giddy: | Shaky / stupor / uneasy stomach / happy |
| 'Gin: | Do over |
| Goozle: | Throat / Adam's apple |
| Gunnies: | Flour sack / tote bag made of burlap |
| | |
| Haids: | Heads |
| Hoochie-koochie: | Questionable women |
| Hydrophobe: | Hydrophobic / animal disease |
| | |
| Iffen: | Perhaps / maybe |
| Innards: | Stomach / gut |

| | |
|---|---|
| Jist: | Just |
| Kettle: | Pot / pan / large cask |
| Kilt: | Killed / slain |
| Knoed: | Know |
| Larnin': | To learn / have learned / will teach |
| Likker: | Moonshine / whiskey / beer |
| Lil': | Small / tiny / short |
| Loos'a: | Turn loose of something |
| Lye Soap: | Homemade soap made of ashes, lard, and lye |
| Membered: | Thought of / remembered |
| Mite: | Maybe / insects of birds |
| Mitta: | Should have done / maybe |
| Mosied: | Went along / gait / sauntered |
| Nary: | Nothing / nil / nada / zilch |
| Nigh: | Approaching / entering |
| Nuff: | Enough |
| Offen: | Often |
| Outs: | Mad at yourself / out of sorts |
| Pilin': | To stack / lay upon |
| Piller: | Pillow |
| Planks: | Wood / lumber |
| Poach'in'em: | Go where you shouldn't / encroaching another's territory |
| Polecat: | Skunk / dirty dog traitor / rotten to the core |

| | |
|---|---|
| Potty Brigade: | Everyone has to go to the bathroom at one time |
| Purty: | Pretty / attractive / lovely |
| Reckon: | To think of doing / believe |
| Red Lite: | Questionable section of town / hangout for ruffians |
| Rite: | Right |
| Ritely: | A good thing |
| Scairt: | Scared / frightened |
| Shore: | Yes / sure |
| Skivvies: | Underwear |
| Skooch: | Move closer to / move away |
| Smak: | Hit / whack / kiss |
| Spade: | Shovel / digging implement |
| Straiten: | Straighten |
| Sumthin': | Something |
| | |
| Tarn: | To turn |
| Thangs: | Things |
| Thay: | They |
| Thay'll: | They will |
| Thet: | That |
| Thum: | Them / those / they |
| Toards: | Toward / approaching |
| Trien: | Trying |
| Tomorrie: | Tomorrow |
| Tweren't: | Wasn't there / was not going to be |
| | |
| Warsh: | Wash / clean clothes on a clothes line |
| Werms: | Worms |
| Whar: | Where |
| Whar'd: | Where did |

| | |
|---|---|
| Whilst: | While doing something |
| Whizzin': | Flying / buzzing / humming |
| Wiff: | With |
| Wimmen: | Women / ladies / young girls |
| Winder: | Window |
| Whut: | What |
| Whut'er: | What are you doing? |
| Whut'll': | What will you do / think |
| Wurst: | Very bad |
| Wus: | Was |
| Yore: | You / far away / long ago |
| You'enses: | a group of people |
| Youngins: | Little kids / babies / children |

This word guide is for any of you that may have difficulty in understanding hill talk. If you will slowly pronounce a word in question, the phonics of that word will often sound the way it appears as written. These are just a few hill talk words, otherwise I would be writing a complete book on hill talk. Happy reading!

By the way, I am aware that the usage of "me and Tut" instead of "Tut and I" is grammatically incorrect. I chose to use the dialect in the stories to preserve the speech of the era. Correcting my father's speech would have been grossly impertinent and highly disrespectful.

# PROLOGUE

For you to understand the nature of these stories, you need to understand why and how I came to write the stories of my first book, *Windy John's, me 'n Tut* and this book, *Windy John's, Rainbow and the Pot of Gold*.

I began to listen to Daddy tell stories about his childhood when I was a little girl and found them to be fascinating. I could close my eyes while sitting on his lap and visualize a mountainous region filled with various types of people living in log cabins and maintaining a living from the soil. It was as though I could drift back in time to place myself in the atmosphere of living without electricity, running water or the natural use of man-made luxuries that we merely take for granted.

Daddy spoke about all the hill folk and how everyone chipped in when the going got rough to survive. They were like a very large extended family. If one hurt, they all hurt. In fact, most of them would give the shirt off their backs to a soul in need. That is, if they had a shirt to give away! For many of the hill folks it was a pleasure to receive hand-me-down clothing. They were not too proud to wear them. There were no closets full of clothes nor did you choose which dress to wear or trousers to put on. It really didn't matter if someone wore the same thing all the time.

What did matter, though, was how they extended a helping hand. They showed love and courtesy for their fellow man. That was the objective.

For entertainment, well, that was a moot subject. A body made do with whatever was available. Many times, they would play dominoes or checkers, hide and seek, or simply find themselves in a big mess of trouble, which of course seemed to gravitate toward Daddy and Tut. They didn't go looking for trouble, but their penchant for being rotten little devils and playing pranks would land them into hot water practically every day.

Since there was no electricity, there was no TV. They didn't sit around wondering what they would do next. As they lay in the sleeping loft, they automatically plotted the next day's strategy. It appeared, even though they were not twins or blood relatives, their minds worked in the same fashion and on the same brain waves. Daddy said it was almost eerie how they could hone in on the same thought and how their instincts for trouble and dastardly little deeds would create havoc. He said it was their way of surviving boredom. They learned quite quickly and understood the nature of life.

Anyway, all of these stories passed along to you are because of a promise I made to him. For a while after he had cataract surgery, Daddy came to live with my husband and me. His diabetes urged a healthy lifestyle and he defiantly balked at my instance to insure a proper diet. His quote to me was, "I had one momma and I don't need another one to tell me what to do." He didn't appreciate not being able to eat whatever he wanted, when he wanted it. Under major protests, he went home!

About two years later, not taking his medication and gradually becoming less able to fend for himself, the nursing home, where he could surround himself with people his own age, seemed to be the only alternative we had.

He naturally was not pleased when the key to his beloved old truck no longer was available. He thought his independence as a man was in question. In order to keep his spirits alive, I would drive him wherever he wanted to go and visit with him daily.

It was at this time when he became less interested in his surroundings and his zest for living was waning. I requested him to tell me all the stories he could remember about his childhood. Many times, he would drift back in time, only to cry or laugh at some of the crazy things he did. That was when his stories began.

Why I am writing them now? Well, I promised Daddy, before he passed away, that I would write his stories for everyone to enjoy and crossed my heart never to divulge the true stories from the fiction. That's why I am sharing his love for living and the stories of his childhood. It's my gift to Daddy.

Although Daddy and I sat for many weeks laughing together and often shedding a tear or two about the nature of his antics and why his devilish ways seemed to attract trouble, he said with a twinkle in his eye, "Well, I suppose God gave me the ability to unearth the mystical habits of nature. It allowed me to experience all the joys of living. Growing up in the hollers, I found life was a simple process. You didn't need all the money in the world to be happy. The one thing people miss out on today is not experiencing the joys of an imagination or having a hero. There are too many things to distract the mind. Most people are too anxious in obtaining the future right now. They don't have time to sit down and realize the future is now, not tomorrow! Tomorrow will get here soon enough and unless you store up good memories about the yesterdays, the tomorrows won't mean a thing."

I remember profound words repeated by Daddy. He often said, "Don't say you don't have time to do something important. That's a crock! Remember this and you will always have time on your hands. There's more than seven days in a week! There's today, yesterday, the day before that, the day after that, tomorrow, day after tomorrow, the next day, a day after, two days ago and now. All of those days bring you right back to the day you started. People need to remember the past to live in the future. The past is a dream to make the future a reality."

Anyway, let's get on with the stories....

# RAINBOW AND THE POT OF GOLD

One morning when Pa needed to go to Grampaw's house, I naturally traipsed along to play with Tut. It had been a couple of days since we were able to get into trouble and I was having withdrawal symptoms from the separation syndrome.

It was a crisp cool morning; abnormal for the beginning of the summer months. The breeze felt good as it whispered in my ears. We decided to take off across the field instead of walking down the lane. I thought we were merely taking a shortcut through the woods, but I found out Pa's reasoning when we approached a massive group of sweet aromatic Wild Violets peeking out from under the shade of wide berthed oak trees. Green moss was clutching the north side of the trees, displaying a backdrop of soft beauty for the delicate purple blooms and the air filled with an aroma so enticing it beckoned a closer look.

"Ain't this the purtiest site? These lil' Violets are like yore Ma; soft and gentle but shore nuff strong in spirit," Pa said as he knelt down on his knees, "this is yore Ma's secret garden. She planted one lil' Violet fer each of you youngins when you were born. Now look at'em; thay're growin', jist like you."

Pa took his pocketknife in hand and laid an old handkerchief across the damp, dew-kissed ground. Plunging the large knife blade into the soil, he carefully extracted a clump of Violets, making sure to not destroy the root system. Pa placed them gently upon the handkerchief. "Yer Ma said to fetch sum fer yer Grammaw. One thang, J.D., this ain't no place to brang yore friends. Unnerstand?"

17

"Ok, Pa." I understood what Pa was saying and respected his wishes. I didn't tell a soul about Ma's very special place ... not even Tut.

After a few minutes reveling in the quiet atmosphere, Pa and I went on our way. It didn't take too long to reach the house, and I was anxious to see Tut. Since Pa would be there for a while, we could go to the duck pond and skip rocks or play with a make-believe town in the roots of the old Hackberry tree. That was such fun! The roots of the Hackberry tree had, over many years, forced the root system upward in search of needed rain. They appeared as mountains with a royal gorge between each root system and allowed our imagination to run rampant, pretending houses and stores were built between the valleys. We used strips of bark for bridges and twigs for fences. Mounds of dirt mixed with water and grass dried like adobe brick; allowing us to carve out areas for doors and windows. We had our own make-believe town and knew one little world was actually at our feet.

My anticipation for fun was nipped in the bud! Tut was feeling puny and Grammaw wouldn't even let me sit on the bed. "Nope," she said, "ain't no rhyme nor reason fer Tut ta pass along the croup. Yer ma don't need you youngins to git sick. Ya best be gittin' outside afore I plaster yer chest wiff mustard oil."

Because I didn't like the old mustard plaster and didn't want to get sick, I told Pa I was going to go exploring and I wouldn't be gone too long. No telling what I would find in the woods. If Ma could have a secret garden, there had to be more secrets out there – somewhere.

For the most part, I had been all over the hills, except for the top of the hill above Mr. Matlock's general store. That was my direction, and the results left a profound structure to remember. It didn't take too long to wind my way around the hill, and I didn't anticipate what came next.

"Don't take no wooden nickels, son."

I felt hot sweat pop out on my forehead and my skin felt clammy. I wasn't alone! I turned around in search of the voice but didn't see a soul. The last thing I heard before I made a hasty exit from the crest of the mountain was, "Don't take no wooden nickels son." The hair on the back of my neck was standing at attention as my feet slid down that hill in record time. Who the heck was that and what in thunder was wooden nickels? I can guarantee you one thing; I was 'running' a one-man marathon posthaste and I swear my feet didn't even touch the ground until I got home. In fact, I didn't even say a word to anyone until Pa came home.

Around noon, Pa came walking through the backdoor. He was greeted by Ma, "Thar's sumthin' wrong wiff J.D. He ain't said nary a word. Ya best be checkin' him. He's out yonder, sittin' on the choppin' block."

"Er ya feelin' poorly?"

"Don't ritely know, Pa. I done had the beejeebers scairt rite out of my senses. Pa, I been hearin' voices! Thay're talkin' 'bout wooden nickels. Twudn't be so bad but I nary saw a soul and all I could hear rumblin' around in my brain wus, wooden nickels, wooden nickels, wooden nickels."

Pa started laughing and said, "I see ya done met up wiff old Red Willet. He's a mite strange but iffen he wus yellin' 'bout wooden nickels, I reckon he musta been seein' a reflection of himself. Why, he won't hurt ya. He's as good as gold."

When Pa was serious, he never lied. He might kid around at times, but I could always tell when Pa was serious. A very thin line formed across his brow and his eyes became soft. It was as though you could see straight through to his soul. I felt at ease and would later return to meet Red Willet.

About one week later, I told Pa I was going to find out about wooden nickels and see the man who was nothing more than a voice. I reached the top of the hill and stopped where I had heard the voice. Many vines intertwined among the trees and shrubs, hampering my vision by their density. It took a few minutes to finally catch a glimpse of an old creaky, dusty house overtaken by gnarly vines attaching themselves to any loose piece of wood.

When I adjusted my eyes from squinting, to my surprise, there on a creaky old wooden porch in a cane-backed chair sat a stooped, wrinkle-faced little man. In my mind, he had to be at least ninety years old, and to tell you the truth, I wasn't certain if I wanted to get close to him. His hair was white with red streaks and sleeked back into a braided pony tail hanging almost to his waist. His eyebrows were bushy red with wayward white hairs jutting in different directions; almost as a symphony of fine musicians fused together in harmony. His white eyelashes seemed to fade inside the sagging, drooping eyelids, but they couldn't hide the gleam in the color of his sky blue eyes.

I couldn't help but notice his left hand was missing three fingers and a very large scar on the palm of his right hand had pulled the bony fingers into an arch. Odd white freckles dotting his leathery, sun-tanned face appeared to play tag with his scraggy mustache as a smile came across his face. It took me aback. His smile delivered an almost toothless canyon mouth. One lonely upper tooth glinted in proud reverie; exposing itself like a fine painting.

After a few seconds, I heard myself say, "How'do? My given name is John but jist call me J.D."

"Thet's a rite good name. Ye can call me Rainbow."

"Pa said yore name wus Red Willet."

"Yup! Thet's fer legal stuff, but to my friends, like you'n yore Pa, it's jist Rainbow!"

"Why? Is it yore nickname; like mine is J.D.? How'd ya git thet name?"

"Been chasin' rainbows all my life. Thar ain't nuthin' I mitta tried. Why, I been to Californie searchin' fer gold durin' the rush, rode trolley cars, fought Injuns, sailed the seas to Chinie and gatherin' wooden nickels; searchin' fer thet pot'o gold at the end of the rainbow. Thet's how I got my nickname."

"Pot'o gold? Ya mean ta tell me thet at the end of a rainbow; thar's a pot'o gold? Jist whut is a wooden nickel? How'd ya lose yore fingers? Whar is Chinie? Whut brung ya to the hollers?" I was full of questions and couldn't wait to hear his answers.

Rainbow shoved his bony fingers inside his pocket and pulled out a hand full of wooden nickels, "First thangs first, youngin'! Back time ago, these here wooden nickels were jist a joke. Thay wus given to people jist like me who didn't have enough sense to come in from a drivin' rain. Lots of times when a body bought somethin' thay thought would be good, it turned out to be nuthin' but wood shavin's thet looked jist like seeds, spices and some times even meat. Iffen ye wus stupid to believe ye wus gittin' whut ya bought, thay gave change in the form of a wooden nickel. Many a time I bit down on a piece of wood thinkin' I got my money's worth. Bitin' down on thet stuff rattled my brains a couple of times and cracked my teeth afore I had the gumption to figger it out. I reckon thet's why I have so many of the danged thangs and why I jist got one tooth. Gold? Well, it shore nuff depends on how a body thinks about gold. These here wooden nickels could be gold, cause thay are full of memories. Thay ain't worth nothin but I hold on to them cause thay represent my life: a life full of wonderful experiences. Each one is like a mirror. All I have to do is close my eyes and see the excitin' thangs I've been able to do. Ain't ya ever heard 'bout a pot'o gold? Thar's a big pot'o gold at the end of every rainbow. Trouble is, the rainbow jist goes on fer ever and ever. I heard tales of men thet hunted fer years hopin' to find the elusive gold nuggets but wound up jist like me wiff the wooden nickels. J.D., iffen ye will ponder about it fer a few minutes, I reckon yore brain will hone in on the meanin' of wooden nickels and the pot'o gold. "

Rainbow and I sat there for hours talking about things that made my mind whirl. When Rainbow was twelve years old, he decided to leave home. He was the sixth sibling of thirteen brothers and sisters. His ma died after the last baby was born and his pa never could decide what he wanted to do: be a father or just take off for the wild unknown. Rainbow's eldest sister took care of the kids as best she could, but it was hard for her to be ramrod for the entire family.

Food was scarce; hunger pangs terrible. His last memories of the day he decided to leave were taking an old shotgun and ammo, some dried beef jerky, a canteen of water, matches and bedroll and walking out the door. Tears flowed but he never looked back. In Rainbow's words, the past was history.

Rainbow didn't know how many miles it took to catch up with a wagon train. He spoke of beating a six-foot rattlesnake to death with a rock and nearly freezing to death at night. I remember Rainbow laughing when he said the reason he didn't use his shotgun to kill the snake was because the rock was closer to him and he didn't want to waste shells or because it was from being cold or just plain scared.

Rationing the water was the hardest thing to do because the salt from the beef jerky left the tongue desperate for water. He prayed constantly for someone to come along or to get a glimpse of a passerby in the distance. He thought at one point that he would surely die but his will to live was greater, far surpassing giving up his ghost.

Finally, when he thought his destiny was to be alone forever, a wagon train appeared on the horizon. He said he was so excited that breathing became difficult and his head felt as though it was full of air swishing around inside his ears, cutting off the instinct to hear.

Oxen-driven Conestoga wagons with wide wheels and

canopied tops and many people came upon Rainbow as he stood there in the baking sun.

Dusty and dry-mouthed, he began telling them he got lost from his family while hunting for food. He told them he probably wasn't missed because of his large family. He wasn't sure that they believed him, but who was going to question a kid standing in the middle of nowhere, all by himself?

A young man and his wife who were searching for a better life in the west opened their arms to Rainbow. They made sure Rainbow was given good care and respected. He happily rode shotgun for this young couple and knew that whatever happened in the future would be up to him. By the grace of God, his group of the wagon train made it to California. There were those in the train who were tired and drifted off in different directions and those who found their peaceful sleep under a lonely tree or amid the vast sea of grassy plains. Rainbow's will to survive would take him on journeys of a lifetime.

For several years, I visited old Rainbow and grew to love this gentle man. He spoke of panning for gold in the valleys of California and how many people died because of hunger, panic and greed that consumed the life of overzealous men.

Rainbow held up his hand and said that his fingers were shot off simply because he picked up a gold nugget he had found. Some man, deciding that he wanted to jump Rainbow's claim, tried to take the nugget from Rainbow. As the two fought, the nugget fell back into the water. Reaching down to retrieve the nugget, Rainbow said the man lowered his shotgun, fired two blasts and blew his fingers into the water. At that point, Rainbow didn't care if he never found another piece of gold.

His right hand was injured while on a cargo ship, en route to China. A very large hook used to hoist cargo slipped and pierced the center of his hand. He was dangling in midair with the cargo, wondering how many hands he would have to lose before he got enough sense to settle down. He made a promise to himself that if he ever got back to California, he would never get back on another ship.

There had to be a better way to live! It was by accident that he settled in the hollers. He had tired of the wanderlust going from place to place, town to town, never knowing where his last days would be spent. Venturing toward the south, he stopped to rest from his journey on top of this hill; he felt a quiet peace overtake his soul and knew this would be his final stopping point.

Rainbow told me many stories, and after several years of visiting with him I could see the resemblance between the two of us: vivid imagination and a desire to learn. We laughed and cried together and shared secrets as he taught me that life has many avenues. The avenues come to forks in the road and whatever fork I should decide to take, make a decision; don't look back but ahead for better things.

One morning Pa gently shook me awake to tell me that old Rainbow had died during the night. My heart sank and I cried like a little baby. My wonderful, gentle friend was gone. As I wiped my tears, Pa placed into my hands a mound full of wooden nickels, each one of them gently carved with, To J.D., From Rainbow, my ... Pot'o Gold.

\*

*I wrote the following song for my Daddy in memory of Rainbow.*

# WOODEN NICKELS
© Joyce Rapier

Verse:
Don't take no wooden nickels I heard the old man say.
You can't get nothin' for'em, even on a rainy day.
I didn't understand the old man on the porch,
as he rocked back hard in that old cane chair
and he said it loud once more.

Chorus:
Don't take no wooden nickels, son, no wooden nickels please
You can't get nothin' for'em 'cept a little girlish tease.
Don't take no wooden nickels, take instead old wooden lore
Cause another wooden nickel is as wooden as the one before.

Verse:
Don't take no wooden nickels kept rumblin' in my mind
I wondered what that old man meant as I left him far behind.
That night I asked my poppa 'bout what the old man said.
"It's because that old man likes you, son,
he sees you in the life that he's led."

Verse:
The old man and I, through the years, became the best of friends
He spun tales'o gold, of fishin' holes, and kite streams in the air.
Blue trolleys rollin' down, dusty broken cobblestones
of river floats, calliopes and the wooden nickels in his coat.

Verse:
Don't take no wooden nickels became a part of me
because of the wooden nickels the old man gave to me.
I'm glad I took the time for the wrinkled old man's prose,
As a child I liked the nickel, as a man I cherish it most.

Repeat Chorus

Tag:
Cause another wooden nickel, son, is as wooden as the one before.

# OFF THE MOUNTAIN

I've told you about Grammaw and how she loved the great outdoors and most living things. "Don't'cha dare hurt them lil' critters. Why, thay have a rite to do a powerful livin' cause God poked'em here to balance out the nature of thangs. Iffen ya go about livin' the way yer supposed to live, nature will take care of ye."

However, one thing Grammaw didn't like; snakes. Snakes, Grammaw thought, were the pure devil himself. One day while Grammaw was over at our house visiting with Ma, their conversation turned from everyday chitchat to when Grammaw was going to move, down from the mountaintop. "Ye ain't gittin' me offen thet mountain. Ain't nuthin' but the likes of snakes, whutt'll make me fold up my bedroll."

Now, Grammaw shouldn't have said that aloud. Grammaw knew we wanted them to live with us, but she was as stubborn as our mule, Old Joker. When her mind was set ... it was set! Or so she thought! She didn't count on the fact that Tut and I overheard what she said to Ma, and boy, was she in for a surprise. If Mohammed didn't get down off the mountain, the mountain, with a little help from me and Tut, was going to make a believer out of Mohammed.

Tut and I set our little plan in motion. While Grammaw was visiting with Ma, Effie Mae and Aunt Sukie were tending Baby Jo. Pa and Grampaw had gone to town. They wouldn't be back for a while, so we knew we had to get things done in a hurry.

We told Ma and Grammaw that we were going to Mr.

Matlock's store and maybe take a swim in the creek. We had gotten our chores finished and we wouldn't be away too long. Ma told us to be careful and to stay out of trouble. We convinced them we would be back in a couple of hours and not to worry.

While Tut went to the barn to fetch a gunnysack, I went to the woodshed and got a long pole that Ma used to stir the fat renderings when she made lye soap and a long-handled grubbing hoe. We would use the grubbing hole to turn over rocks, and the pole for gouging into holes where we thought the snakes would be hiding. The only kind of snakes we wanted to find was little green grass snakes. We just didn't realize what was in store for us.

Tut and I hurriedly went to Grammaw's house. On the way up the hill, we turned over some very large rocks but didn't find one single, solitary grass slithering, slant-eyed snake. We did manage to find scorpions with their tails curled over their backs and ugly old black centipedes with hundreds of orange legs. We knew those things could sting the pure devil out of a devil's advocate but decided to catch a few, just in case we didn't find any snakes. We scraped them inside the gunnysack, very carefully, but lost count after the tenth one. In fact, we weren't sure how many of the tail stingers we actually put inside the gunnysack. All I know is that it was too danged many!

About three-fourths of the way up the hill was the biggest old green snake we ever thought of finding. Since the green snakes weren't poisonous, I cautiously reached down and grabbed it behind the head. I tried to poke it inside the gunnysack. Its old tail was coiling around my arm and I knew it wanted to bite me. The bite of a snake could make a body go into rigors. Since Tut didn't like snakes, but was willing to do whatever was necessary to get Grammaw to move into our house, he grabbed the snake by the tail and held it in midair while I opened the gunnysack. Kerplop, into the gunnysack went the snake.

Figuring we wouldn't find any more snakes, we went on up to the house. We laid the gunnysack down and proceeded to plot another scheme. While we were sitting on the front stoop of the house, wondering what we could do, Tut started fidgeting and backing up very fast. His butt was scooting on the wood planks so hard that I knew if he didn't stop, he'd get a piece of wood shavings rammed up his butt. He kept lifting his butt up in the air while his legs did the crawdad dance. Soon his hands started pounding the floor and sweat began pouring down his face.

I looked at Tut and said, "Whut'er ya doin? Er ya havin' a fit? Say sumthin', Tut!"

Tut looked at me with his mouth slightly askew, trying to muster up a sick little grin and said, "Sumthin' went up my britches. It's a crawlin' inside my skivvies. J.D., ya gotta look fer me. I'm a feared it's liable to bite off sumthin' I might be a needin'."

Trying to get Tut to be still wasn't very easy. I sat down on Tut's head and began to open the fly on his britches. I must admit we looked funny and sure was glad nobody was around to see what happened next. The minute I unzipped his fly, I nearly had a heart attack. Out popped the head of that old green snake. I jumped off Tut's head and headed to the other side of the porch. Tut was lying there in a frozen state while that old snake slithered up out of his britches, over Tut's chest, down around his neck and then crawled through the front door. As Tut stood up, his pants fell down around his ankles and he was walking toward me, taking little tiny baby steps.

"Tut, whar'd thet thang come frum?"

"Shore nuff don't know! Ya reckon it crawlt out frum under the porch? Check the gunnysack. See itten It's the same snake. J.D., I think I done messed my britches. I ain't huntin' no more snakes! Grammaw can live up here if she has a mind to, but I ain't a sleepin' whar snakes crawl up britches!"

I walked over to the gunnysack, gently opened the top and peeked inside. Sure enough, the green snake was still inside but some of the scorpions and centipedes were gone. In fact, it appeared that every one of them had crawled off where they could hide. Just as well! The snakes were giving us one fine fit, and if there was one snake, you could bet there was at least two more from where that one came. One snake had already crawled into the house, and we figured that it would be the one to get Grammaw to move off the mountain. Anyway, I tipped up the gunnysack and turned the green snake loose.

Instead of going inside the house to look for the snake, I picked up the pole and digger and flung the gunnysack over my shoulder and we headed home. Tut's bony legs were still a mite shaky from the snake crawling into his skivvies, and he was ready to find a place where he could sit down safely and forget all about slithery snakes and the reason that threw us into this situation. If Grammaw wanted down off that mountain, she'd have to do it on her own or stay up there with the snakes.

About halfway down the lane, I could feel something crawling in my hair. I told Tut to have a look. It might have been a spider, since we had gone through some spiderwebs while turning over all those rocks. Tut looked but didn't see anything. I just shrugged it off and figured it was just my imagination. We took a few more steps and something began to move across the hair dangling from my forehead. "Tut, thar's shore nuff sumthin', ticklin' my head. I reckon to tell ya, now, I done unzipped yore drawers, the least ya can do is find out whut's in my hair!"

Tut looked at me and said, "I think I best n-n-not tell ya wh-wh-whut ya got stuck up yonder in yore hair, J.D."

"Tut, pull on yer tongue and stop thet infernal stutterin'. Jist take yore hand and knock it outta my hair. It cain't be all thet bad."

Instead of Tut knocking it out of my hair with his hand, he grabbed up the long pole and began whacking me across the head. He whacked me so hard I was beginning to see stars. Then he jerked the gunnysack off my shoulders and began stomping the daylights out of every square inch of that gunnysack. I though he'd had gone nuts. He was screaming his fool head off, saying, "I ain't touchin' th-th-thet thang!" Then he began to yell, "Ma! Grammaw! Ma! Grammaw!"

All of a sudden, I could feel something creeping up the nape of my neck. I knew something other than spiders was hanging in my hair. I wasn't exactly sure what it was, but I knew if Tut couldn't talk straight, tried to do bodily harm by whacking me on the head, and then turn deadly on an old gunnysack, it had to be danged serious.

Ma had heard Tut screaming and she came running towards us. She took one look at me and told me to stay still. She reached down on the ground, picked up a stick and flicked out two big old scorpions. When I realized what had been in my hair, I could feel the blood drain right out of my face.

Ma asked us where we had been and how two scorpions managed to crawl into my hair. The only thing I could think of saying was, they must have fallen from a tree. Dumb!

She told us, "Go to the barn, strip yer clothin' and shak'em out real good. Don't ya be a bringin' yer bodies inta the house iffen ya have any more scorpions hung in yer clothes. Ya can jist stay out thar all nite long!"

Grammaw said she and Baby Jo needed to go home. It was about time for Grampaw and Pa to get home from town and she wanted to start frying some taters for supper. She told Tut to get on home in a few minutes.

Luckily, Baby Jo had fallen asleep. Ma told Grammaw to leave her at our house; Baby Jo could spend the night with us. Lucky little Baby Jo! At least she wouldn't have to be in the house with the green snake.

Tut told Grammaw he'd go on home with her and help her with supper. Tut said they had gone into the house, fixed supper and never once saw that green snake. When Grampaw got home, they sat down and ate their evening meal. Tut said he had one eye on the floor and the other eye looking toward everything else. Tut figured the green snake had slithered out the door and he didn't have to worry. That evening everything seemed to be just fine. They sat around playing dominoes until it was time to go to bed.

Tut said he looked under his bed, threw off all the blankets and searched high and low for that green snake. Grammaw and Grampaw went to bed. In a few minutes, they were sleeping soundly. That is, until Grammaw had the urge to use the chamber pot.

She reached under their bed, pulled out the old tin pot and, by the light of the moon flickering through the window, could see something moving inside the chamber pot. Thinking it was a shadow inside the chamber pot, Grammaw began relieving until something touched her backside.

Tut said she stood up real fast, let out a scream, jerked up that chamber pot and flung it across the room. All its contents and the snake smacked the sidewall so hard that Grampaw came flying out of the bed. Grampaw was soaking wet with pee and Tut knew in an instant that Grammaw found the snake. Tut said that Grampaw grabbed up the lantern, lit the wick and screamed, "Woman are ye tryin' to drown me er whut?" Tut told how he wanted to laugh out loud but knew if he did Grammaw might have flung him against the wall with the snake and he had had all the snakes he wanted for one day.

The rest of the night Grammaw was sitting in the rocking chair waiting on daylight. At first light Grammaw was packing everything in the hay wagon. The mountain had finally moved Grammaw!

We spent six whole days moving and rearranging beds,

fixing another place for a cook stove, bringing critters down from the small mountain pasture, calming the old sows not wanting to let go of their wallering holes, and all the while Grammaw was looking for snakes.

Well, Tut and I would like to have taken credit for getting Grammaw down off that mountain, but since we couldn't, we were just enjoying being a very large extended family and knew the mountain was smiling.

# HUMMERS

It seemed as though Tut and I were supposed to be living together. Since we had been together since Tut's mother died, we thought of each other as brothers. We knew we weren't blood kin but somehow Tut and I could hone in on the very same thought at the very same time! It was very strange how the image of his likeness could reflect my very own person. We didn't look that much alike, except for the devilish glint in our eyes. Our thought processes were almost identical. Our thought process would get us into deep, deep trouble!

One day while Pa and Grampaw were in town, Grampaw saw some very pretty, tall red flowers growing in a flower garden. There were masses of them, in bloom near the south wall, gracing the old red, dirty brick frame with a majestic statement of grandeur. Since Grampaw wasn't shy, he knocked on the front door and asked the lady if he could have a start of the flower. She gladly gave Grampaw several of the tubers and told him to cut off the massive green leaves, plant them just below soil level and water them well. In the spring, the gigantic flower would begin to bud, and before long, he would have more plants than he could possibly want.

Because Grampaw didn't know the name of the flower and wanted to surprise Grammaw with the gift of the plants the woman told Grampaw they were cannies. All the way home, Grampaw kept saying, "Cannie, cannie, cannie," so he would remember how to pronounce it when he gave Grammaw the flowers. I came to find out later that the name was cannas.

Grammaw had the greenest thumb and could grow most anything. She already had coreopsis, wild mountain lilies, flags, daffodils, wild buttercups, purple bee balm, blackeyed susans, hollyhocks, and many other wild flowers that grew on the mountainside. When Grammaw decided to move down from the mountain, she dug up nearly all the plants. She carefully transplanted each flower along the perimeter of our house. It looked so beautiful when they were all in bloom. Anyway, when Grampaw got home with the plants, he was grinning from ear to ear and said, "Lookie here whut I brung home. Why, these are the purtiest red flowers I ever did see and thay'll bring the hummers rite up to the winder."

"Whut'er thay called, Pa?"

"Canines, Ma."

"Ya mean to say it's a dawgs tooth?"

"I reckon. Thet's whut the lady said. Ya best be a plantin'em cause thay need to be in the ground come winter."

Grammaw was so proud of her new canines and hovered over them like a little old red hen giving care to newly hatched chicks. She warned us all, "You youngin's stay out of the newly planted flowerbed. Don'tcha be a diggin' in this flowerbed fer fishin' werms. Iffen ya have a mind to go a fishin', ya better do yer diggin' somewhar else! Ya done been warned. Iffen I catch ya undoin' whut I jist done, yer backside'ser gonna git tanned. I shore nuff want to see these here canines grow tall so's the hummers will drink out the nectar, come springtime!"

Grammaw was a sassy little thing, no bigger than a peanut but could pack a wallop as hard as any man cause me and Tut's backsides had been on the receiving end of fine little switches stripped from a tree by our very own hands. She could make a believer out of the devil himself, especially when she yelled, "Go git me a switch. Ya better git a switch thet's got a fair bit'o bendin'. Iffen I have to go fetch a switch, I might be a bringin' a log."

We should have realized, after all the rotten, devilish things we were prone to do, and did do, that staying on the right side of Grammaw was surely the best way of preventing those skin burning, biting, bitter stings of a hickory switch. However, Tut and I just couldn't control our propensity for creating nasty little pranks.

All winter long, Grammaw would go out to the flowerbed. She would check the progress of the "canine" flowers. She would gently lay mulch across the tubers as though she was caring for a newborn baby, pat the ground with the tenderness of an ingrown toenail and pretend to be conversing with someone she had known for many years.

Finally, after a very cold winter, spring had started to awaken the long dark months of sleeping trees, grassland and flowers. Vibrant and jubilant colors leaped from the flowers. The trees were the first to show signs of life and then daffodils purged from the earth to blossom into a vast yellow array of colors with an enticing aroma. It seemed that daffodils and little yellow flowers were always first to bloom, before the trees had a chance to completely leaf out and destroy the sunlight needed for them to leap into the limelight. The mountain lilies, as if taking a cue from the daffodils, would arouse the tender bulbs into fruition and compete with the affection from Grammaw.

True to form, the hummers showed up around the middle of April. Hummers would migrate to the area in search for sweet nectar. The delicate nectar would fuel their little bodies for many days of flight.

Usually Grammaw would put out sugar water in little tiny containers, placed in various places so everyone could enjoy the antics of near collisions in winged flight attacks. They would stay around awhile until they began nesting and not appear again until the baby birds fledged from the nest. Then the hoopla began. Some of the birds would be very aggressive; others would be submissive.

At last, around the end of April, the "canines" began to emerge from their sleep. The warm blanket of the soil encouraged growth and they obliged. Tender young shoots from the dormant tubers would heave the soil, as if they were in an anxious hurry to show Grammaw their loveliness.

It seemed as though they would never stop growing. Those tender young shoots turned into enormous tall stalks, as massive leaves began to creep into view and unfurl into draping fronds. In short order, the blossoms began to break into some of the largest red ruffled flowers Grammaw ever saw. She was so proud of those "Canines" and could hardly wait for the hummers to return with their newly hatched brood.

Enter me and Tut! Remember about the corn likker still we found in Frog Holler? Now what we did next was a dastardly little deed but at the time we thought it would be the best way of catching one of those little birds. All we wanted to do was see one up close. They were like little dive bombs and could fly faster than you could blink your eyes, zip around your head with an energetic vengeance and sound like they were spitting out profanity with every die doe. As hard as we tried, we couldn't catch one of them to save our sanity.

One morning, Tut and I set off to find something to entertain our boredom. Our ability to think was stifled. Since we had worked so hard the previous day, Pa and Grampaw told us to have some fun. "Go fishin'. Build ye a tree house. Why, thar's plenty of old planks frum the rebuildin' we done. Fetch some'a the wood un go hammer fer awhile."

Tut and I thought that would be a great idea, so we toted some wood, hammer and nails and set out for the back portion of the pasture near the base of Frog Holler. Since the tree was fairly large and there was no easy access to the nearest tree limb, we took some of the planks and nailed them, one by one, until we had a make shift ladder of sorts, all the way up the tree trunk. Very carefully, we climbed the tree and decided which limbs would be most suitable for the tree house floor. While we were sitting on one of the large limbs, I told Tut to go back down and start handing me the old planks and I would begin nailing them to the tree. We hammered the planks until we completed the floor in a large vee of two big branches.

We sat there awhile purveying the masterpiece. It was our own private little tree house. We were proud of our accomplishment and knew we would have a great time. We could peer over the pasture and spy on anyone who happened to be near our secure world, high above the ground.

Zoom, bitzt, zoom, bitzt! Hummers were all over the place. They were dive-bombing around our heads in a fierce defense attack. That's when our brains turned to mush. We were going to catch a hummer. We didn't rightly know how, but we'd figure some way.

As usual, Tut was getting hungry, so I told him I would go get some biscuits and jowl. Tut yelled, "J.D., fetch one of the mason jars. Jist don't let anyone see ya do it."

We hurriedly got down from the tree and I ran back to the house and snatched an empty mason jar. Ma stepped out the back stoop and wanted to know what I was doing. "Nothin', Ma! Jist wanted to git a couple'a biscuits and hog jowl. Tut and I had a cravin' flung on us fer jowl. It's ok, ain't it, Ma?"

"Why shore, Honey. You'enses be careful and don't git inta any trouble."

I scooted back to the tree with the biscuits, jowl and Mason jar.

"Tut, whut ya need the mason jar fer?"

"Well, I figger we need to warsh down the biscuits with sumthin'. Let's traipse up to the corn likker still. It might taste purty good."

Tut and I set off for the "corn likker" still. We knew we had to be very careful or risk having shotgun pellets in the butt for trespassing on forbidden grounds. Taking extreme care, we sneaked through the woods. We were trying to alleviate making any type of noise: stepping on twigs or making rocks fall from their resting places.

We tiptoed up the path. Gingerly, we crept slowly, slowly, toward the big keg of mash. Tut took the gourd hanging near the keg and scooped up enough "corn likker" to fill the mason jar. With our hearts pounding through the excitement, I cupped my hand over the mouth of the jar to keep from spilling the liquid and we made a hastily exit from Frog Holler.

We sat down at the base of our tree house and began feasting on our snack and drink. Knowing we had more "corn likker" than we needed to be drinking, Tut took a drink and I took a drink. Well, maybe we took more than a drink or two. By the time we were finished taking sips, there was just about one-fourth cup of "corn likker" left. We were feeling a mite warm and a little bit giddy.

"Ya know sumthin', Tut? I shore nuff don't like this stuff. I keep 'memberin' the last time we got so sick and I'm feelin' jist the same way now! We best not move very fast or we're liable to be a heavin'."

We lay there for nearly two hours before we had enough sense to remember our own names. If "corn likker" makes us feel so stupid, what would it do to hummers?

Tut and I stood up, looked at one another and realized we finally had a way of catching a hummer. We walked back to the house pretending we were as innocent as two patron saints. We sneaked to the flowerbed and poured the remaining "corn likker" down inside the large red flowers. We put the mason jar away and walked into the house. We wanted to know what everyone had been doing while we were away. Did we miss anything while we were building our tree house? Innocent little devils we were.

Grammaw decided to sit on the front porch and watch the hummers. She sat, patiently waiting for a few minutes. Sure enough, four little hummers went straight for the nectar in the big red flowers. Dipping their long beaks into the flowers, they began sipping the "corn likker" nectar. They would sip a little bit, fly straight up and go for another sip. It didn't take too long. The hummers began to feel schnockered. They would try to fly up in the air but couldn't get any farther than the long leaves. They sat there for a few seconds and plopped down to the ground. All four of them!

Grammaw saw this entire happening and ran to the hummers. She gently picked them up and cradled them in her hands. "It's them damned old canines. Thay done kilt my hummers. Why, them thangs must have the pisin in'em!" She laid the hummers on the seat of her rocking chair and began jerking the "canines" out of the ground with the vengeance of a mad woman.

Dirt had landed on Grammaw's face and at the same time "corn likker" had flown from the giant red flower and landed square dab on Grammaw's lip. She stopped dead in her tracks, licked her lips, turned around with blood and daggers shooting from her eyes, lips pursed tighter than a tick on an old hound dog, grabbed up a good-sized board, kicked a metal bucket across the porch, flung open the screen door and headed ... God help us, straight in our direction.

"Thomas Uriah! John Dean! Git yore butts in here. Ya best not be a hidin', cause I'm fixin' to set ya both on fire."

God help us! Grammaw was on the loose and madder than hell. When she started calling us by our full set of names and screaming like a banshee, we knew we were about to meet our maker.

Before we knew what had happened, Grammaw got us both in a headlock; pushed our heads together, bent us over her left leg, shoved her right leg over our backs and with our heads dangling toward the floor, raised her right arm up over her head with a board clinched in her fist like a vise and wailed the dickens out of our butts. When she got through whacking our butts, she pinched each of our ears and jerked us through the front door.

We appeared as though we slid through a meat grinder. Our butts were hotter than fire, our ears were the size of basketballs and the top of our heads had dirt and "corn likker" ground in and matted together like glue.

Everyone in the house had come running to find out why Grammaw was faunching at the bit and why we were pleading for mercy.

"Ya see them thar lil' birds? Ya best be a lookin' right good and a heedin' my warnin'. Iffen airy one'o thum lil' birds kicks the bucket, yer gonna need a damn big old wench to pull my foot outta yore butts! Take thum lil' birds and nurse'em back to the way God intended. Ya best be a prayin' fer'em whilst ya git to the flowerbed and replant my canines. Iffen airy one'o thum don't poke thar heads back up towards the heavens, ya both'er gonna have to live in your tree house. Whar'd ya git the corn likker? Ya been messin' and nosin' and a gaumin round agin, ain't ya? Do the two'a ye boys know who yer a messin with? Don't be a crossin' yer fingers behind yore backs. I ain't gonna settle fer nuthin' but the truth!"

After we told Grammaw. First fib: "We sneaked the corn likker frum yer piller. Shucks, we nary knowed it wus so powerful. We didn't figger the pain a little drop would do!" Notice.... We didn't mention a thing about Frog Holler!

We cleaned up the flowerbed while smiling through our teeth. We gingerly looked over our shoulders for the sight of Grammaw. We didn't want to see her coming toward us. Another pinched ear and we wouldn't be able to hear for a week. We didn't like that one little bit!

Nursing the hummers (thank you, Lord) back to their healthy little dive bombing nature, we told Grammaw the second fib: "Why, we jist wanted to get a closer look at a hummer. Why, thay'er the cutest lil' thangs. We jist wanted to git a better look. Gosh, Grammaw, we shore nuff didn't think the likker would make'm giddy'er schnockered."

As we stood up to eat our supper and apologized for being such rotten two of a kind, devil may care brats we managed our third fib: "We'll never, ever, do anythang bad like this agin!"

As we smiled and kissed Grammaw on her cheek, we put our hands behind our backs and half-heartedly crossed our fingers.

We knew in our hearts and mind that what we did should never be repeated, at least, anything that had to do with Grammaw, hummers or "corn likker."

# MICE, MICE AND MORE MICE

It's not so much what we did but how we did it. Trouble was knocking on our door. This day in particular wasn't any different for our antics; it just snowballed into a giant fiasco!

Effie Mae and Aunt Sukie were playing house in the barn. They had dolled up in some of Ma and Grammaw's old clothes and donned hats from Grammaw's collection of hand-me-downs. Some of the hats came from her mother and some were homemade from the skilled craft of fine needlework.

One hat, a creation from a collection of old timey buttons and feathers, a genuine designer special was favorite. Each button and feather, attached to an old piece of flour sack, had tiny hand stitches securing them in place with a masterpiece design. Other hats were similar to bonnets, which looked as though they may have come from women settlers.

You could almost envision sturdy women wearing the wide-brimmed bonnets shaded from the glaring sun sitting in covered wagons. A child protected by one arm and the other arm wrapped snuggly around a shotgun as the family crossed the wild unknown. They were dependant on one another in their quest for a better life.

The dresses Effie Mae and Aunt Sukie chose to wear were too large. That was because at one time, Grammaw was a large woman. Not in height. She was pudgy around the mid-section. Those were her I-et-too-much-whilst-we-wus-crossin'-the-plains dresses! "We et cus ... we feered dyin'. The fat purt near kilt me un I sweared to the good Lord, iffen He'd see us thru the danger'o Injuns thet everbody wuz fearin', swelterin' heet un freezin' cold, I'd git the fat offen my belly. Shucks, I nary saw one Injun. I figgered thay wuz as scairt of us as we wuz of them and didn't want no part of us. Thay twern't bad folk. Thay wuz only trin' to proteck whut belongst to them. Iffen airy a soul tried to harm any of you'ins or try ta kill our only meat source, I reckon Pa 'n Grampaw would go on a rampage jist like the Injuns did." True to form, Grammaw kept her word.

Anyway, aromatic cedar and Lavender permeated the fibers of the dresses. A lingering scent hovered over animal dung. Believe me, the mixture of cedar, Lavender and animal dung would choke a horse! The bottoms of the dresses, adorned with pieces of flour sack where they had been worn threadbare from many days of use, dragged the dirt floor of the barn with each step they took. Sometimes when they would take a step, their feet would tangle up in the dresses and whammo, face first, down in the dirt they'd go.

They were pretending to be fine women, talking to one another as though they had good sense. I am quite certain that the pictures from the Sears catalog had a lot to do with how they were acting.

Those pictures could take you away from the everyday doldrums into a make-believe state of mind and deposit you right into the catalog, leaving you with a wish list. Dumb females. It seemed to Tut and me that making a wish list was a powerful waste of time. After all, according to them, they did housework all the time, and in my way of thinking, playtime shouldn't involve or revolve around the same old thing. They should be doing something else. Something to broaden the mind and get the creative senses flowing.

The girls had spread an old cloth across a makeshift table and placed some of Ma's pewter plates, old tableware, mason jars, a jug of 'tea' and a plate full of Ma's sourdough biscuits onto the table for what they called a 'tea party.'

Not real tea, mind you. We didn't have real tea very often and when we did, it was for special occasions. When a craving was flung upon us for tea, we would drink Sassafras tea. Sassafras is a small laurel tree with a statement. You knew immediately, when one of the branches snapped, releasing a faint whisper of camphor, you had found a Sassafras tree.

We'd take a spade and dig the roots, shake off the dirt, wash them, let them thoroughly dry, and then boil the roots. Doing so made a light shade of pink tea. For some reason, we couldn't dig the roots until the month of March, when the sap had just started to emerge into the root system. Then we'd set out to dig the new shoots from the runners of the tree. To this day, I can still smell the sweet aroma and taste the lasting flavor.

Normally the consumption of Sassafras "tea", used for a "good cleaning out" was in the month of April. Old timey folklore thought it cleansed the blood and purified any kind of germ lurking in the body. Many people thought Sassafras tea thinned the blood and was a necessary ingredient in a diet. Some thought it was to insure that sluggishness didn't interfere with doing hard work during the summer. Whatever the reason, people drank the tea because it was right in their backyards, literally. For some, it was a nuisance because the roots would spread at a rapid pace and be almost impossible to remove. Our family didn't have time to worry about slow blood or being cleaned out – the adults made sure we didn't sit on our rumps too long.

Anyway, those gooty girls would sit around their table, pick up those mason jars, stick their pinky fingers out to the side of the jar, sip "tea" and nibble on the sourdough biscuits. Naturally, crumbs from the biscuits would drop on the dirt.

Enter – me and Tut and mice! Tut and I had hidden behind a pile of hay and had been watching the entire show. We knew it was just a matter of time before the girls would climb up the ladder into the loft and then all hell would break loose.

You see, Tut and I had been collecting mice. They were just little baby field mice, no bigger than an index finger, but they were critters. Critters that liked to chew. In fact, they would chew anything that didn't chew back. Tut and I had been feeding the little mice pieces of sourdough biscuits. Boy, they liked those sourdough biscuits. In fact, those little mice had gotten larger than we had anticipated and weren't afraid of us. Some of them would eat out of our hands and would crawl up our backs to perch upon our shoulders. To tell you the truth, it had gotten a little out of control. It appeared the mice were telling other mice; aunts, uncles, cousins, brothers, sisters and grandparents – go taste the sourdough biscuits.

Well, as I said, it was just a few minutes before the girls climbed into the loft – for the last time. They were using the loft as a bedroom for their "babies." Their babies were old sock dolls made from of the upper portion of Pa's socks. The embroidered face of the dolls had eyes, a nose and smiling lips and yarn for hair. The bottom of the dolls was just the opposite. There was an embroidered frown to show an unhappy baby. They had wrapped the old sock dolls tightly inside small homemade quilts. With love and care, Effie Mae and Aunt Sukie laid their babies on the hay.

As they gingerly climbed the ladder, Grammaw's hats precariously perched across the brow of their heads and sourdough biscuits in hand, they took great care, knowing each step they took would trigger the long dresses in a tangled mess.

Effie Mae said, "Well, I reckon we best check on the babies. It's nigh time fer'em to be a needin' changin' and feedin'."

Aunt Sukie was the first to step into the loft. She scooted the hay around and then sat down. Effie Mae, following suit, managed to dangle her long legs over the edge of the loft. She reached over and scooped up one of the baby dolls in her arms. "Is this here lil' baby mine? Thay look jist exactly alike. Jist two peas in a pod. Turn'em upside down: why, thay still look alike." Both of the girls started laughing so hard, tears were streaming down their faces.

Aunt Sukie, trying to contain her laughter, said, "Like Ma allus says, iffen I knew then whut I be a knowin' now, this here lil' baby would'a been fully growed afore I had her. Ya know sumthin', Effie Mae? I reckon not to be havin' real babies ... thay make a powerful stink. I ain't ritely fond'a changin' them poo poo holders cause it makes me gag."

Once again the girls began laughing and kicking the floor of the loft. I have to admit, the way they were talking and what they were saying was extremely funny. Tut and I had to make a hasty exit from the barn before we split a gut holding back the laughter. We finally sneaked back in the barn just in time to reap the rewards of patience.

Effie Mae and Aunt Sukie were sitting there so serenely, singing to their babies, gently swaying their arms to the tune of a lullaby, when Aunt Sukie said very tartly, "Git yore laig out frum under my dress. Ya keep a movin' inta my space. Ya know I ain't abidin nobody inta my space. Skooch over!"

"I ain't got my laig under yore cock-eyed dress. By the way, iffen ya stick yore hand toards my back agin', I jist mite smak ya."

As Effie Mae turned around to reiterate the fact, she wasn't doing anything wrong, her face turned ashen and she let forth with a bloodcurdling scream that sent shivers up the spine. Because she was dangling her feet off the loft, she had nowhere to go. She tried to scoot backward into the loft. Hard as she tried, she was stuck in the scream mode. She wouldn't shut up. Aunt Sukie was trying to find out what was wrong with her and why she was screaming, when, all of a sudden, the cold fact and reason came scampering across her lap, en masse.

One of the mice had perched itself on top of Effie Mae's hat and then leaped on the front of Aunt Sukie's dress. Aunt Sukie sat there in a frozen state, unable to make a peep. It was the first time Aunt Sukie was speechless. Kerplop. Aunt Sukie melted right into the hay. She had passed out. Not realizing the magnitude of what was taking place, Effie Mae placed her hand down on the floor loft to get needed leverage to stand, when, of all things, one of the mice ran up the dress sleeve. She was flailing around worse than a chicken doomed for the chopping block.

Aunt Sukie finally aroused from the passed-out stage, only to enter a wild panicked, frenzy. Her eyes widened, her mouth popped open, sourdough biscuits and mice began flying through the air. She kicked hay from hell to breakfast. Cautiously reaching over to pick up her baby doll, one of the mice poked its head out the top of the quilt. That doll turned into a heap of scraps as she whacked the daylights of everything in her way. She stood up, mice hanging from every nook and cranny in her dress, and came to realize a mouse was eyeball to eyeball, staring at her from the neck of her dress, which had, in all the excitement, inched itself up around her mouth. Hard as she tried, the top of that dress was stuck to her mouth like glue. It wouldn't go up, it wouldn't go down, and the mice were hanging on for dear life. She tried to scream through the lacy collar of the dress, but for the first time in her life, her mouth plastered shut.

With a big whack, Grammaw's feather and button hat went flying through the air, landing upside down near the rafters of the barn. Mice were squeaking to high heaven and running for their dear lives. It's no wonder. Aunt Sukie's long blond hair was sticking out as if she had seen a ghost and hay dust was all over her face. She was a holy mess.

Effie Mae, managing to jerk her old bony legs up over the rails, turned over on her belly and with her knees firmly on the loft floor tried to stand up. The front hem of the dress had hooked itself onto a sliver of barn loft and it was wedged firmly in place. She couldn't get the dress out from under her knees and was twisting it from front to back, trying to figure out why she couldn't move. The more she tried to free herself, the more entangled she became. Hay was sticking out of her hair, giving her the appearance of a Sweetgum ball. With a little bit of tinsel, she could have been an ornament on a Christmas tree.

Finally, both of the girls managed to get their footing and began the hasty descent from the loft. Effie Mae put her left foot on the top rung, clinched her baby doll between her teeth with the baby quilt dangling around her neck, missed the last four rungs, and fell three feet to the dirt floor. When she hit the floor, her feet squashed several piles of freshly dumped cow dung, making her do the splits. Her splits splattered the stinking mess up the inside of her dress. She tried to wipe the dung off but made matters worse when the baby quilt dangling around her neck dipped into the smelly poop and smacked her in the face. She looked like something the cat wouldn't bury!

Aunt Sukie, peering from the loft, was so startled at the sight of Effie Mae that she completely forgot about the lacy collar around her mouth. She began to sputter, "Ger mer durrn." I do believe she was trying to say, "Git me down."

Throwing caution to the wind, knowing full well that whatever transpired within the next few seconds, good or bad, Tut and I emerged from behind a pile of hay. Our intention was helping her from the loft.

Before we could take a step toward the ladder, one of the mice ran under her dress. She began doing a wild dance, tripped over her own feet, slid on a piece of sourdough biscuit and was coming down the ladder, head first. Her legs had gripped around the ladder tighter than a cock-eyed vise. Her dress turned inside out while hanging down around her head. She looked like one of those two-sided flip-flop dolls. One flip, you saw one doll, and flipping the skirt over you saw a different doll.

Tut and I began to yell in unison, "Tarn loose'a the ladder.

Ya ain't got too fer ta fall. We'll catch ya, jist tarn loose." Finally, convinced we would catch her, she uncoiled her legs, loosened the grip of her hands and gently slid down the ladder, head first. Right into our arms. Once her feet hit the dirt she flew out of that barn. She had one hand waving in the breeze and the other hand jerking the bottom of the dress away from her feet. Boy, did she boogie.

Although this little escapade lasted for only four or five minutes, you can bet it was the highlight of our day. Believe it or not, the result of feeding those little mice turned out to be one of the funniest three-ring circuses we ever did see and it was all free – thanks to sourdough biscuits and mice!

# THE POWER OF UNCONDITIONAL LOVE

I don't believe there's anything more heavenly than to sniff the cool night air as it gently kisses the cedar trees, dances like fairies across pond water and brushes against bitter weed grasses. Lying in bed at night with the windows wide open, you get a nice warm feeling as the cool breeze whistles across the brow of your face as it sneaks a peek beneath the covers. It makes a body sink further into the downy fibers of a homemade mattress, knowing in your heart Ma and Grammaw's quilts would warm the very soul and secure a peaceful night's sleep.

There's absolutely nothing in this world worse than to sniff the cool night air and get wind of the aromatic wonder of a skunk or polecat, as we called them, cranked up, going ninety to nothing, without an emission control. The odor created a sickening havoc for those in peaceful slumber. We rattled out of a good night's sleep. Awaking to moans and groans of everybody in the house was like hearing ghosts in torment.

The nose would automatically shut down. We placed pillows and anything handy across the face, sort of like a facemask: to eradicate further ingestion. Our eyes would begin to burn and smart, with tears streaming down the face and lungs heaving in mighty roars of hacks and coughs, and the stomach would turn over in gags and barfs. Things only got worse when a body in deep desperation took facemasks off to alleviate suffocation. That, in turn, made the whole process futile. Damned if you do and damned if you don't!

You see, our neck of the woods, so to speak, was crammed full of all kinds of critters. Two of the critters, The Great Horned Owl (we called them Screech Owls, because when they made a noise, it sounded like someone scraping their fingernails down a chalkboard) and PooPoo De' Stink, (skunks) were bitter enemies. It wasn't so much that they were enemies, but survival of the fittest made sure they were not on somebody's dinner plate.

Mind you, the skunks wouldn't hurt the owls, but the owls would scarf down the skunks' whole body and regurgitate bones and fur into little heaps beneath their nests. Sometimes the owls would use the fur to line the nest for soon to be baby owls. In fact, walking through the woods, you could find piles of bones and fur from the owl feast. One swoop of their mighty claws and a skunk was history, except for the stink! Since the Great Horned Owl can't smell a cock-eyed thing and skunks can't fly, the only thing a skunk can do is release the putrid, stomach turning stink in hopes that the owl won't swoop down and gouge out his gizzard. Wrong!

Well, this little tormenting stench went on for nearly three weeks. None of us was getting any sleep and our sunny dispositions were beginning to turn sour and defensive. Each morning, we'd awaken to find ourselves trapped in the midst of grouchy, touchy, snippy remarks from cranky family members. We all smelled worse than Gertie's drawers and couldn't stand the sight of one another. It was touch and go – you touch me and out you go. Literally! We had more sponge baths with lye soap than I care to remember and no amount of vinegar or tomato juice smeared on the hair would get rid of what was ailing us. Outside air didn't help one little bit. Everywhere you went the stench was overpowering, and every breath you took was like sucking down rotten eggs. We were stuck in a stink hole with nowhere to go.

Finally, Pa and Grampaw decided to find out where the stink

was lurking. With rags wrapped around their faces and socks over their hands, they set out in search of the dastardly, little, vile, juice squirting, black-and-white striped varmints. To tell you the truth, it wasn't because they wanted to. It was because Ma and Grammaw were in such foul moods, threatening everyone with bodily harm and refusing to cook, that lit the fire under Pa and Grampaw.

I overheard Pa tell Grampaw, "Them wimmens shootin' bluddy fire frum thar eyes. We best git to findin' thet critter afore we starve to daith. I'm shore nuff gittin' tired a eatin' dumb old cold biskits. Don't ritely know which of them females is the wurst. Fire shootin' or stinkin' puke shootin'."

Grampaw said, "We best split up. You go toards the bottom side of Frog Holler and I'll scope out the barn and out buildins'. Yell fer me iffen ya find the critter. Don't fergit, the thang mite be a foamer. One bite frum a foamer'll give ya hydrophobe."

Pa and Grampaw looked high and low for that polecat and decided they would just go back home. They were empty-handed. They were plum tuckered out and sat down on the front stoop trying to catch their breath. All of a sudden, Grampaw stood up real fast, jerked Pa off the stoop and told him to be quiet. Grampaw was a real big tall man and to watch him tippy-toe in clunky old boots was a remarkable sight. "I done figgered whar thet polecat is a hidin'," he whispered to Pa. "It's under the stoop."

Pa gingerly sneaked over to the stoop, laid his head sideways on the ground and cautiously looked under the planks. The slope and darkness under the stoop prevented Pa from seeing the full scope of hidden things. He began crawling on his belly toward the center of the porch. He backed out from under the porch and told Grampaw to get a spade and two gunnysacks. "It's a bit more than we done bargained fer."

By that time, Ma, Grammaw, Effie Mae, Aunt Sukie, little

Baby Jo, Tut and I had crowded around the porch. We wanted to know what was happening. "Did'ya find the polecat, Pa? What'cha need the spade fer? Whut'er them gunnies fer? We were chock-full of questions and weren't getting any answers.

Pa told Ma to get us kids back in the house. Pa didn't want us to see an unpleasant sight. Grammaw stayed outside and helped Pa remove the culprit who had been giving us the dickens.

Of course, me and Tut sneaked back outside and watched what the grown-ups were doing. Grampaw handed Grammaw one of the gunnysacks and she placed the open end on the ground. Pa scooted a very large mamma skunk inside the sack. The poor little thing was severely injured. It appeared to have had a gaping gash around her lower mid-section and was nearly dead. What was even more of a shock was the sight of two baby skunks. They were barely alive and still trying to nurse their mother.

Grammaw wrapped the baby skunks inside the clean gunnysack and headed toward the barn. While she was taking care of the baby skunks, Pa and Grampaw dug a small grave and buried the mother skunk. It appeared that the mother skunk stayed alive until her babies were safe and then simply passed away.

Tut and I raced toward the barn. Grammaw was there, sitting on a milk stool, tears streaming down her face, saying a prayer for these little baby skunks. Beside her was a small pail of cow's milk, tilted sideways to provide easy access to the milk. Dipping her fingers down inside the milk, she'd rub the noses of the baby skunks. She would tickle the hair under the nose and around their mouths in order to encourage them to suckle. At least, she hoped they would drink droplets of milk from her fingers.

Seeing Grammaw tenderly caressing those baby skunks made us realize how blessed we were to have a Grammaw full of compassion and loving tenderness. Tut and I sat there full of awe and filled with perfect love for our Grammaw.

As Tut and I decided to leave the barn; only Grammaw, knowing in her own special way that the two of us had been watching, yelled for us to come on in. "J.D., Tut, git on in here! I need ta be a tellin' ya bout these here lil' baby skunks. Pull up a chunk'o hay and sit yore selves down. Well, boys, I reckon ya knowed the momma skunk died – but do ya unnerstand the powerful meanin' of why'en how the babies survived?"

Tut and I stared at one another and all we could do was shrug our shoulders. We knew about the love and tenderness we had just witnessed. It was a scene forever etched into our minds. We also knew about the love for our family but didn't understand what Grammaw was trying to do. She wanted to unearth from our minds a greater form of understanding.

Grammaw continued, "A momma's full'o love fer their babies. It don't have to be a human momma. A momma is a momma even in the animal kingdom. Th' momma of these here lil' babies gave the most lastin' love of all. She died fer'em. Pore lil' thang musta been in a fierceful fight, but the thang she remembered most wus her babies. I reckon she knoed to fill the air with her scent. Maybe she wus tryin' to tell us to take care of her youngins. I guess whut I'm tryin' to tell ya is – love ain't got no boundries. I reckon you boys will jist have to help me feed these here lil' babies to make'em grow."

Tut said with a lump in his throat, "Grammaw, thet's whut my momma done, ain't it? She knoed to git back whar the love wus a flowin'. I rekon she gave me and lil' Baby Jo a good thang to remember' afore she died." Until this time Tut had never really said anything about his momma. It made us all cry.

Tut and I threw our arms around Grammaw's neck, squeezed her with all our might and promised to help with anything she wanted. We were going to be nursemaids. We dubbed the little boy skunk Butterball and the other one, a little girl, Stinky.

In our haste to do anything Grammaw wanted, we didn't have enough sense to realize the time consuming ordeal we had been snickered into doing.

However, a promise was a promise, regardless of the circumstances. Besides, those little baby skunks needed a momma and we were going to find out in due course exactly what being a momma entailed.

Since Butterball and Stinky were just babies, probably two to three weeks old and no bigger than a good-sized sweet potato, still reeking of a major stench and in need of food every few minutes, we devised a plan and set it in motion.

Whew, the both of us still had the aromatic perfume stuck to our clothing and weren't allowed back into the house until we had a full-blown bath, so we decided to stay in the barn until the skunks were big enough to fend for themselves. It wouldn't have done any good to take a bath because we kept handling the babies and the babies in turn would lay the stink on us, all over again. The prospect of winning this battle of stinks was futile, to say the least.

That evening, Pa brought a coal oil lantern and matches, two plates chock-full of fixings for us to eat, as well as a bedroll to spread down on a stack of hay. We tried our best to smooth out that hay – but hay is hay, and regardless of what we did, we wound up with hay sticking into our butts, throughout the night. It didn't matter much, because every two hours those little skunks would make throaty little noises in search of food.

Each of us would take a shift in feeding the babies and then try to get some shuteye. We didn't mind feeding the skunks, but it left a lot to be desired; cleaning up the runny, mushy piles of backside yuk. The first time we had to scoop up the mess wasn't too bad, but each interval of cow's milk created an undesirable digestive disturbance. You could almost see their digestive juices churning. Those little stomachs would begin to growl and roll, rock back and forth like Grammaw's old cane chair and then, without warning, the tail would hike up and spew green and black goop. It was enough to make a body turn inside out. Tut and I had the dry heaves all night long.

Just the sound of one of us gagging made the other one turn a light shade of puce green. I guarantee you one thing – looking forward to several weeks of wiping green and black goop off a skunks' bottom was not a favorable or pleasant experience.

The next morning everyone came out to the barn. Ma had food for us and the girls were anxiously waiting to see the baby skunks. As they stepped inside the barn, their eyes focusing in adjustment to the darkness of the barn, all of them began to laugh their fool heads off. Tut and I were peering through bloodshot eyes. We looked and felt like a cornfield scarecrow. Each of us was holding a baby skunk in one hand, tightly cupping our mouths with the other one and hoping for a miraculous intervention from God.

Grampaw, sauntering towards us, said, "Did ja find any grubs'er crickets?"

"Grubs? Crickets? Whut about grubs'en crickets?"

"Grubs'en crickets to feed the babies!" Grampaw said with a snicker.

"Ain't nobody said ary a thang 'bout grubs'n crickets! We been a feedin' em cow's milk!"

Grampaw gently took us aside and began to lay upon our feeble minds a powerful lesson: of wisdom. "Well, boys, ya still got a ton a larnin' to do. Ya see, them lil' baby skunks done been taught to grapple in the dirt'n fend fer themselves. Even tho' thar Momma wus nursin'em, thet wus only temporary to the thangs whut made'm grow. Growin' is larnin' patience and seein' the broad scope of thangs. It ain't all jist one color. To be knoin' the truth ya gotta seek the answers. Yore Grammaw knoed the two of you would be a hankerin' to care fer the babies and figgered to larn ye a lesson 'bout the whys and hows of bein' a momma. She knoed ye both would be gittin' sick of the feedin' and cleanin'. Grammaw knoed iffen ye survived the night with these here lil' baby skunks, jist feedin' em cow's milk, ye could shore nuff see the job through by showin' the baby skunks whar'un how ta find the grubs."

Tut and I sat there in silence. Grampaw's words of wisdom cut through us like a hot knife slicing a chunk of butter. We had just experienced a taste: newly found humbleness. Whatever it took, we were anxious to fulfill our promise to Grammaw.

For the next few weeks, Effie Mae, Aunt Sukie, Baby Jo, Tut and I turned into full-blown surrogate mothers. Everywhere we went the baby skunks would follow. As we turned over old rotten logs to expose various bugs and grubs, the skunks would take their powerful long claws and dig into the soft soil to unearth tasty treats. They managed to grow very quickly and were playful with each of us. They would run at us, pat their front feet on the ground, raise their tails high above their backs and back up. Not once did either skunk attempt to spray us with the aromatic perfumed flavor of the night.

One morning, as Grammaw said would happen, they disappeared. We knew in our hearts, for one brief moment in time, the meaning of love and the hows and why a mother's love is unconditional.

# CHIGGERS, MOSQUITOES & LYE SOAP

Boy, it was hotter than hell outside and not much better in the house. The cook stove always had coals in the belly and the smoke belching from the flue added to the uneasy, stifling air. Sweat poured off our faces and our clothes dripped with underarm perspiration. Sometimes we'd strip down to our bare necessities, but no matter how hard a body tried, there was just no way to get cool. Maybe a dip in the creek would soothe the skin for a while but the sun beating down on the water would create a reflection on the water and blister the skin unmercifully. You couldn't go anywhere to get cool. There was no breeze to fly across the face because the trees just stood there with crackling leaves curling up from lack of rain. Going barefoot was not tolerable because the grass beneath our feet crunched with every step we took.

The bugs, those God-awful bugs, wouldn't die. They were everywhere. They delighted in basking in the heat and seemed to multiply faster than we could swat them. Swarming around the body, alighting anywhere a piece of skin was available, made a body angry, miserable and downright unpleasant. They chewed the patience right down to a nub.

All of us kids were nitpicking at one another, edgy and ready to knock off each other's block. It was like eating razor blade soup. We had sharp barbed tongues, were hateful and the slightest thing would set us off in a rage tantamount to a volcano spewing. We were out to do ourselves a mischief.

It didn't take long before we were in a full-blown fight. Effie Mae said Aunt Sukie was an old grouch and the race was on. Aunt Sukie chased Effie Mae into the cow pasture, grabbed her by the hair and tackled her to the ground. They were plastered with cow dung and weeds. Tut and I were in hot pursuit. We laughed and said how they were stupid old females. Both of the girls stood up, dripping with dirty sweat, mushy old cow poop and stinking to high heaven. Before me and Tut could take a breath, they took cow dung and threw it all over us. It splattered all over our faces, up our noses and hung in our ears. It took us off guard, and while trying to gain our composure, the girls came running at us, knocking us backward into an old wood and rock fence. It was a good ten minutes before Pa and Grampaw got wind of the ruckus. The sound of their voices quickly put a stop to our shenanigans. However – by that time we had managed to roll all over the pasture into high sticky bug infested, cow dung, chigger loaded weeds.

We called a truce and headed for the creek to wash off the stink, gunk and bugs adhering to our clothes. Ma made us stay outside until our clothes were dry and our little perfumed bodies stopped reeking. We had managed to get into one fine mess. None of us realized the magnitude of our fracas until several hours later.

It was about dusk and still as hot as ever. Ma said we could sleep outside for the night – if we promised to stop fighting. Of course, we promised not to fight. We'd stay close to the house. We hauled our pillows and some blankets to the front stoop and made pallets on the old hard wood planks. The mistake we made was not taking off our dirty clothes. Another mistake we made was putting the pallets too close together.

We had snuggled down for the night and were enjoying the stars flickering in the dark sky and seeing an occasional firefly light up the night. It was shortlived.

Aunt Sukie was moaning about something whizzing around her face – then Effie Mae. They were shuffling about like two old sows, kicking the blankets off me and Tut and sitting upright scratching the daylights out of their legs. It was a constant scratch. You could hear fingernails gouging the scalp and each of them was saying, "Scratch my back. Down, jist a little bit. No, yer missin' it. Go up further." It was contagious.

Tut kept yelling, "J.D., stop a ticklin' my face. Don't cha be doin' thet agin'. Sumthin's itchin' my laigs! It's whizzin' round my haid. It's a bitin' real bad. It's them durned old blud suckin' skeeters."

I have to admit they weren't the only ones who were itching. I was clawing at my butt and around certain areas that shouldn't be clawed. All of a sudden, a mosquito sat down on my ear lobe and bit the living hell out of me. It laid an itch on me so bad that my ear swelled up the size of a hornet's nest. My ear was on fire and it felt like someone had whacked me in the head with a board. I could feel my ear burning but soon forgot about it when my other ear was attacked in a feeding frenzy. A mosquito was lodged inside my ear and buzzing like crazy. I jerked the covers up around my head so tight that I couldn't breathe. When I jerked the covers up, I exposed the bare ankles to the blood sucking varmits. They hovered over my legs like buzzards looking for a good, juicy meal.

Aunt Sukie and Effie Mae were fanning the air trying to shoo the mosquitoes away but were not having any luck. Fanning the air created an enormous suction and forced the mosquitoes under the covers. Great balls of fire, we were encased with an itch beneath our clothes and covered on the outside with mosquitoes: lying in wait to devour any precious exposed skin. There was not one square inch on any of our bodies without a whelp the size of a goose egg!

It was the most unbearable night and none of us got much sleep. If we weren't suffering from the unbearable heat, by golly, we were being besieged by night flying bloodsuckers or scratching ourselves raw from the tiny little red chiggers embedded in every fold of our skin.

The next morning was slow in making its delivery. We were anxious to see the sun come up cause we knew the mosquitoes would dissipate and we could bathe with lye soap. What we didn't anticipate was just around the corner and we would soon find out that raw skin and lye soap don't mix.

When Pa and Grampaw got out of bed, we were waiting on them. When they saw all of us lined up, side by side, outside the backdoor, disheveled and peering through bloodshot eyes, it was more than they could take. Grampaw started laughing so hard that tears ran down his face. Trying to laugh, Pa nearly choked on a mouth full of coffee.

Our clothes were hanging on us like a wind whipped clothesline, hair was stuck out in all kinds of directions, our faces were red as a beet, and we looked like knotty, warty toad frogs with giant itchy bumps.

Grampaw hollered, "Grammaw, git the kettle goin'. We got us sum kids whut needs the scrubbin'. Ya best be a gittin' the blak salve offen the shelf and break out the coal oil. It appears the youngins done got a mess of chiggers in thar craks. Th' skeeters done et'em raw! Have Ma bring'em sum clean britches."

We could hardly wait for a hot bath. Pa brought the number ten silver-colored wash tub to the backyard, placed it just inside the smokehouse door, filled it with hot water and gave us a chunk of lye soap. Ma hung a quilt across the entryway. It was to give us privacy. The reason Ma didn't shut the wooden door was to keep us from choking to death on hickory smoke. We had a choice. Itch to death or choke on hickory smoke. Either one of those things might have been a pleasure.

In privacy, each of us stripped down to our birthday suits and waited to submerge our itchy bodies into the steaming, hot water. We were even anxious to suds up with lye soap. The girls went first, both of them standing back to back in the tub. Ma began pouring hot water over their skin as the girls began lathering with the soap. The minute that lye soap hit the raw bare skin, the girls let out a war hoop, "It's a burnin', it's a burnin', it's a burnin'." It didn't take them long to get in and get out.

Tut and I looked at one another and snickered. We shouldn't have snickered cause I am here to tell you, it was no picnic. It was ok until we placed the lye soap on the exposed areas around the lower portion of our anatomy. It literally set us on fire. I don't know which was worse, the itch or lye soap.

After we scrubbed down, Pa came into the smokehouse with the old black salve and coal oil. The black salve came in an old tin can and people used it on everything from a scratch to the toe itch. It smelled like coal tar and was messy and gooey. It was like sticking your hand down in a vat of grease. It also made your clothes adhere to your skin. The coal oil, better known today as kerosene, when applied to cuts, spider bites, and any other kind of bite, eased discomfort. It might have been a stupid thing to use, but when you don't have a doctor close at hand, you resort to old timey medications that are a little out of the ordinary.

Anyway, we rubbed the coal oil on the chigger and mosquito bites and then followed up with the black salve. One thing for sure – we had to stay away from any kind of heat or fire. If we didn't, our clothes would slide off the body or we could have gone up in a puff of glory.

I do know one thing in this world that is a positive. Heat, sweat, fighting, coal oil, black salve, chiggers, mosquitoes and lye soap do not mix!

# BIG LIGHTS &
# OUR BEAUTIFUL SIGHTS

One morning, Grampaw and Pa, sitting under the big oak tree, decided it was time for all of us to go to the big city. Having completed all the chores, what everyone needed was a break from the week-long humdrum of everyday routines. Come sunup the next day, we'd pack the hay wagon with a basket full of eats, pile onto the wagon and head for the city.

All of us kids could barely contain the excitement. We were definitely displaying our very best behavior. Our little treks to the big city were far and few between and to be quite honest, we didn't remember much about the other adventures. I guess it was because we were either too young to remember or it just wasn't something, coining a phrase, 'to write home about.' This time it was different. All of us kids, with the exception of Baby Jo, were most eager to drink in all the visual effects and hold on to new memories. We were growing up and naturally felt the urge to spread our wings. When I say, spread our wings, I mean, spread our wings, not fly the coop. None of us were ready for that ... just yet.

Bright and early the next day, before the sun peeked its old orange head over the hills, Pa and Grampaw secured the mules to the wagon. They piled hay around the inner sides of the wagon to keep anyone from falling off and watched as Ma and Grammaw spread old quilts across the hay for easy sitting. Grammaw had fetched Grampaw's fiddle and placed it on the wagon seat while Effie Mac and Aunt Sukie put the 'finishing touches' on our picnic basket. "Let's git aboard. Iffen ya want to go with us, ya best be a gittin' the lead out," Grampaw hollered.

It didn't take us long to find a sitting place. Ma and Grammaw were at the front of the wagon near the bench seat with their backs to Pa and Grampaw. Effie Mae and Aunt Sukie were on each side of the wagon facing one another. Tut and I were at the rear facing Ma and Grammaw. Baby Jo was in the middle of the wagon. Finally, we were heading down the lane, yelling to the top of our lungs, "Big city, here we come."

Oh, the joy of it all. I shoved Tut's ribs and said, "Ya reckon we might be a seein' some'o them hoochie koochie wimmen?"

Tut stared at me and announced, "Shoot, J.D., even iffen we did, I reckon I shore nuff don't even knoe whut one looks like. Whut do thay look like?"

"Beats me! I heared Pa say thay'er powerful different frum Ma's good looks. I reckon thay must be purty durned ugly. Maybe thay got two haids."

With that said, both of us began laughing and knew right away, this would be something we would never forget. Pa yelled back at us, "Tut, J.D., straiten up yore butts. Ya best not be a thinkin' them thoughts." How in thunder did Pa know what we were thinking?

We rattled down that old dirt road, hitting every rock and bump Pa could find, making us crack our heads against each other. I think Pa was deliberately trying to knock sense into our heads. Actually, what Pa was doing was activating the natural urge to evacuate. Baby Jo was the first to complain. Pa gently brought the wagon to a stop. Ma took Baby Jo to the side of the road. After Ma and Baby Jo climbed back onto the wagon Grampaw yelled, "Iffen ya need to be goin', ya best be doin' it now." Since no one made an effort to exit, Pa started to move the wagon.

I suppose we drove for at least twenty feet when I yelled,

"Pa, I best be gittin' offen the wagon. Don't reckon my bladder's gonna hold fer too long. It keeps a bouncin' round my innards. Iffen I don't git shed of this water soon, my eyeballs'er gonna pop."

Pa brought the wagon once again to a stop. As I was getting off the wagon, Tut followed my lead and the girls plowed over the sides of the wagon and headed to the opposite side of the road. No one ever thought anything about heading for the bushes, especially, when nature called. It was just a natural thing to do.

After all of us climbed on board again, Pa with a disgusted sigh whispered to Grampaw, "It's jist like a potty brigade. If one's gotta go, thay all gotta go. Dangnest thang I ever did see."

We were traveling along pretty good, although going up some of the steep grades was like hanging upside down on a clothesline wire. It might have been ok, except we didn't have a pole to prop up the wire. Ma and Grammaw were sliding on loose hay, towards Tut and me. It wouldn't have been so bad but poor little Baby Jo, in their wake, flattened out like a pancake. Ma and Grammaw outweighed us by several pounds and, with the angle of the wagon – well, it was like shooting a watermelon at a single green pea. Splat!

Clambering along on the dusty old road, Grampaw picking his fiddle and all of us singing and making up songs was wonderful. Along the way, Pa would yell to various people asking how their families were and if they needed anything. That was just like Pa. He was always helping anyone, whether it was giving them food or repairing something that was in need of a hammer and nail.

Before we finally reached the big city, Pa wheeled the wagon to a small clearing and we had the best picnic ever. We spread the quilts on the ground, Pa said grace over the food, and then we enjoyed the feast. A feast lovingly prepared by Ma and Grammaw. We had fried chicken, homemade bread and chunks of potatoes fried really crisp, seasoned with basil and cracked pepper. A jug of water helped quench the thirst. We didn't use any plates – we just used our hands since all the food was like finger foods. After our meal settled, which seemed like forever, we were on our way.

I have absolutely no idea how many miles it was to the city or how many hours it took. All I remember is that it seemed forever. I do remember, quite vividly, when we came to the big steep hill. A big steep hill going down and I do mean down ... toward the city. The hill was very deceptive. One minute the wagon was on a flat surface, and with a blink of an eye we were going, it seemed, at a ninety-degree angle. It scared the living hell out of all us kids.

What was worse? Seeing old cars backing up the hill. Cars got better traction going in reverse. With them going in reverse, it appeared that we were going in the wrong direction. Talk about an optical illusion!

Finally, thank God, we reached the base of the hill. It took a bit of time to go down the hill, because the mules and Pa were slamming on the brakes. It's a good thing those old mules didn't have rubber tires on their feet, because if they did, they probably would still be running or would have had a blow-out and landed in one of the stores.

Anyway, as I said, we reached the railroad tracks at the base of the hill and cautiously crossed them. The railroad tracks were the same line near our crossin'. Looking over to the left, I saw a big majestic red railroad station with wooden walkways. The walkways used for passengers as they boarded the trains were very close to the rails. It made my heart leap in anticipation of other sights we would encounter.

Pa pulled the wagon to a stop near the railroad station, tethered the mules, and we climbed down from the wagon. Parked along the dirt street were automobiles and wagons in front of established businesses. Since we were there for the day,

Pa said it would be best for us to walk down the street and take each shop one at a time.

The first place we visited was a produce store. As we stepped onto the wide front porch, the aroma of sweet-smelling fruit played havoc on our taste buds. Everyone knew this area was a big producer in fruit and the fruit market was thriving with business. People were there to sell their products and, at the same time, purchase fruit, which couldn't be grown in our climate. Pa said we could pick out what we wanted, in limited quantity, when we came back from seeing the other stores.

The next store we came to was a dry goods, general store. Ma and Grammaw were going nuts looking at all the beautiful cotton material.

The material tightly wrapped around wooden bolts beckoned a closer look. Cone-shaped spools of thread were lined up in several different colors alongside funny-looking treadle sewing machines. I could almost see the wheels turning inside their heads. Ma was oohing and aahing as she draped the fine material between her hands, caressing the notion of one day owning a treadle sewing machine to use for stitching pretty clothes from the beautiful material.

There was all kind of toys. Some were made of metal and didn't appear to do anything, while others had wheels and handles and would move with the slightest touch. The girls were looking very intently at baby dolls whose attire was feminine, frilly dresses. It was as though they had drifted into a hypnotic trance and was enjoying flying away from reality to fantasy.

Tut and I were equally in awe of knives, guns, red wagons, and oddly shaped musical instruments. We had virtually stepped into a wonderland of objects – objects only seen in a Sears catalog. I don't believe we ever thought any of these toys would magically appear, but there they were, in full glorious sight.

One of the objects I wanted was a French Harp. Actually, it was a Harmonica, but French Harp sounded more exotic and rolled off the tongue better.

Pa and Grampaw was watching everything we did; gigging each other in the ribs and smiling like a Cheshire cat. They were getting more pleasure watching us than looking at anything else. Unbeknownst to us, Pa and Grampaw were gathering information. Information that would lighten the very hearts, souls and minds for daydreaming little kids and grown-ups.

We could have stayed in that store all day long, looking and drinking in all the wonderful, mind-boggling variety of items. However, Pa said we'd better get along the way, especially if we wanted to see anything else. We reluctantly left the general store and ambled down the street. We were glad we did because there were sights and sounds eagerly waiting to capture and enthrall our curious imaginations.

Situated across the street from one another were two banks. The outside of the buildings, elaborately decorated with massive scrollwork and a shiny red spire topping one of the buildings, caught our eyes. We went inside each of the banks and our mouths gaped open. Beautifully tiled floors glistened with the appearance of shiny glass. The ceilings proudly displayed thin sheets of metal. It was a remarkable sight. Even more of a sight was Pa taking a little book from his coat pocket and handing it to the woman behind a stall.

Going further down the street was a brewery. Now, in my feeble mind, it appeared that if they could brew liquor and sell it, the people in the hollers should be able to do the same thing without getting into trouble. I looked at Pa and said, "Sumthin' shore don't make ary sense to me. Iffen thay can make the hooch and sell it, why in tarnation cain't thay stay outta the woods and stop a whackin' up the pot bellies? Ain't thay got enough?"

Pa laughed and replied, "Well, it's like this. Thay say it's not legal to be a makin'er a sellin', whut ain't taxed. You'n Tut been in them woods? Iffen ya have a mind to go wanderin' whar yore butts ain't got no business pokin' round, ya best mind yer own business cause ya jist might git yore butts shot. Thay'll bury your butts whar thay land cause it ain't no game thay'er playin'. Thay'er gittin' black money fer the fixins' and don't take kindly to bein told thay cain't do whut thay've been a doin' fer years. Jist stay outta them brew woods. Ya hear me?"

I knew Pa meant business. He was serious about one of us being hurt or killed, so I answered him with a firm, "Yes sir, Pa!"

Going further down the street, we came upon a barbershop. Inside the barbershop was a kindly, old gentleman. He was slightly bald and held a pipe in one hand and an old tin cup, full of coffee, in his other hand. The ladder-back chair he was sitting in would teeter and rattle with every breath he took. He appeared to be waiting for his turn in the chair.

Over in a corner was an old black wood burner chucking out warmth as several men, gently inching closer to heat their backsides, conversed about how they were doing and what they expected for the future. If they were generally speaking or just making small talk, it really didn't concern us.

The only thing we were watching was the man stropping a long silver blade against a long piece of leather. He was preparing to shave a man's face and we thought he was about to cut his throat. Tut said in a panic, "J.D, I best be gittin' outta here. I ain't re-re-re-ready ta see him cu-cu-cu-cut thet man's goozle!" In a panic, Tut raced out the front door.

Pa and Grampaw started laughing. Grampaw said, "We best git out thar afore he manages ta git home afore we do."

We saw grocery stores, meat markets, a hotel, drug store, post office, courthouse and a grand building with musical shows. The building where the musical shows garnered attention connected to an area off limit to kids.

The off limit area consisted of a pool hall and a bordello. Fights and drunken brawls were a main feature. Tut and I nearly twisted our heads off trying to see one of those red-faced, hoochie koochie women. We were looking too hard. All of a sudden, one of the hoochie koochie women came sauntering from a side door. A portion of her hair was pinned as wisps of it fell across her bare shoulders. In fact, there was a lot of her skin showing. We didn't know things like that existed. Her lips were bright red and her cheeks looked like she was on fire. She had so much greasy goop on her lips and cheeks that if she accidentally fell down, the grease would have made her slide ten feet. You know something? We weren't too impressed. Pa was right. Not one of those made-up women could hold a candle to Ma. Ma was a true lady and nobody could outshine her beautiful appearance.

As all of us headed back up the main street to go home, we were glad to get in the wagon and sit down. It had been a very long day and we had seen and experienced some very exciting things. As we sat down in the wagon, Pa pitched a bag full of fresh fruit in Ma's lap. Pa winked and said, "Pass'em out, Ma. Here's some sweets fer my sweeties." He reached over and kissed Ma on the cheek, climbed in the wagon and we headed up the big steep hill toward home.

It was getting late and Pa wanted to get home before it got too dark. All of us kids were getting sleepy and we watched the sun as it drifted and finally sank beneath the wooded hillside. After awhile, shadows were flickering and dancing on tiptoes through the treetops. You could see a soft glow from the moonlight. The air was as crisp and clean as fresh falling snow and the stars would twinkle in unison.

As we lay there on the hay, wrapped in the warmth of Grammaw's quilts, we felt the bumps of rocks against the wagon wheels. We heard the plod of the mules' feet against the hard soil. We caught a glancing whiff of burning hickory smoke as it hitched a ride through the air wafting from warm houses in the hollers. Looking up to the stars, we realized the joy and importance in being a part of a loving family. Wanting material things and having warm memories is a natural instinct. However, the most important thing I learned from seeing all the pomp and glory of the big city was the fact that we didn't have to pretend to be something we weren't or fight for things we didn't need.

We had it all – right in our own backyard. Seeing the beautiful starlit sky together – with each other – as a family – was brighter than any big city light. We didn't need the city – we had each other.

# A REAL FAMILY

I suppose going to town should have been the highlight of memories and it was, to a certain degree. Sure, I thought of all the places we saw and all the wonderful toys scattered about on shelves and wandering through the neighborhood.

It filled my mind of how they must live. I wondered, were those grown-ups and children a loving family? Did they sit around, playing dominoes or checkers? Were they able to see life as we saw it and experience nature at its best? Did the children have their backsides tanned when they got into mischief or merely turned loose to run rampant ... in the streets? Were they able to talk with their parents about problems or did they keep deep dark secrets? So many questions raced in my mind, but one question, knocking around in my brain, kept me on pins and needles and shoved me senseless.

For about a week after we got back from the city, my nasty little nature or fondness for pranks couldn't emerge. It was though I was stuck deep in thought, and no matter how hard I tried, I couldn't jolt myself from this deep depression. I felt anchored with questions.

This wasn't normal for me, and everyone around me was noticing the change. I couldn't sleep because of nightmares, and food seemed to trigger an unfavorable taste in my mouth. It wasn't because the food didn't taste good. It was because the worry in my mind didn't allow me to taste anything. I knew what the problem was. It was a deep, dark secret. The secret was eating my mind and bearing ever so heavily on my soul. It needed to be eradicated.

One morning while Tut and Grampaw had gone up on the mountain to check on the old home place, I cornered Pa in the barn. I tried to make conversation, but a lump in my throat wouldn't even let me swallow. My mouth was dry as a desert and words seemed to hang in midair. For the first time in my life, it was a chore to open up my heart and let go of this painful thought I was experiencing.

Shooting the words forth, I said, "Pa, I reckon ya been a wonderin' whut's been makin' me on the outs with myself, ain't ya, Pa? I best be a tellin' ya whut I should'a told ya afore we came back home frum the city."

Looking at me softly, Pa took me by the hand and we sat down on a pile of hay. He placed his big old arms around my shoulders and hugged me very tight. "Iffen ya need to be tellin' me somethin', I figger we can git it everythang all worked out."

"Well, Pa, I best be a startin' frum the first thang thet I knoe fer shore. It's 'bout Tut, but I ain't ritely shore how to spit it out." That old lump in my throat started swelling and I could feel the tears welling up in my eyes. "Ya knoe thet Tut is jist like my own flesh and blud brother. I love him mor'en than anythang, 'cept fer you'n Ma. Our family is the best family in the whole world but I'm feered somethin' mite come betwixt us."

"J.D., thar ain't nuthin' thet could break this family apart. We love one another."

"Do ya 'member 'bout them little skunks. How the momma died and we took care of them lil' babies. It's a shame, Pa, thay growed up never knoin' thar momma or daddy. Whut about the daddy? Do ya ever think he cared 'bout them lil' babies? Iffen the daddy came back ta git the lil' babies, would we have taken the time to nurse'em to grow up, jist to give'm back?"

"I reckon yer trien hard to say sumthin' really important,

J.D., so I ain't gonna say nuthin' till ya git rid of all the thoughts pilin' in on ya. Talk yer heart out and I'll jist listen."

"I knoe me'n Tut were jist lil' kids when his ma died. I have the memories of Lavender spice, the darkness, all the lights round the house, the burin' hole, realizin' she weren't comin' back and the look on Tut's face. Tut don't speak much 'bout his momma ceptin' fer sometimes wonderin' whut mitta been. He loves you, Pa, jist the way I love you. Thet's whut I'm trin' so hard ta say. Whut 'bout his real pa? Do you remember, Pa, when ya told us thet we could go lookin' round the city? Well, don't git mad, Pa, but we mosied down to the hoochie koochin' place. We didn't do nuthin' wrong, I promise! Well, Tut went behind the place to use the privy whilst I waited fer him. Thar was this woman askin' me iffen Tut was my brother. She kept sayin' how Tut looked jist like a lady named Janet. She done asked me all kinds'a questions. Iffen our Ma's name was Janet, whar we was livin', whut we liked to eat and all kinds'a stupid thangs. I figgered it weren't none'a her beeswax'n told her so. All she did was say she shore did miss her friend, Janet and her lil' boy Uri. She told me some man came a lookin' fer Janet and then jist tarned round and walked off. After Tut came back, frum the privy, he said he had the feelin' he'd been thar before. You know, Pa, kinda like the feelin' a body gits when ya think somethin's sneakin' up behind ya. It gives ya the cold shivers. Oh, Pa, my heart is heavy with knoin' – Tut's daddy mite be lookin' fer him. Whar is Tut's daddy? Do ya knoe who he is? Do ya reckon the woman knoes Tut's pa? Iffen he comes back – ya reckon Tut'n Baby Jo will leave us? Do ya think I best be a tellin' Tut? Whut am I goin' ta do?"

It seemed as though I poured out my heart to Pa that morning and actually was afraid to stop talking. I was afraid to find out the truth, but I knew how I would feel if someone kept my pa from me. If Tut's pa was out there somewhere, shouldn't Tut have the opportunity to get to know him and love him? The way we loved Tut, I figured it was like the baby skunks – sometimes, you have to turn loose of love to keep it or risk losing it forever by holding on to it.

   Pa sat there listening to me until I stopped talking. We sat in silence until Pa began telling me what I needed to know. "Well, J.D., I reckon ya had a powerful lot hangin' on yer mind and shoulders. Ye asked some mighty straightforward questions. So, I best be givin' ya the whole truth. Tut is like a son to me. Yer ma and I love Tut, jist the way we love Grammaw and Grampaw and Baby Jo. Thay'er our family. Like I done said, ain't nothin' gonna come betwixt us. I best start frum the day Jennie showed up at yer grammaw's house. Yer ma and I never knoed Jennie 'cept fer the thangs whut we was told. Jennie left the hollers when she weren't no more than a young girl. She was headstrong and never paid no mind to the larnin' whut she needed, to git by in the world. She knoed it all and thumbed her nose at Grampaw and Grammaw. Grampaw and Grammaw didn't even knoe whar Jennie was. Grampaw went to the city one day after Jennie died, and talked to one of the women that lived at the red-lite place. The red-lite place is whar the hoochie koochie wimmen hang out. It's a sad day when a pa has to tell his youngin' 'bout thangs whut should never happen."

   Pa sat there with a sad look upon his face. He rubbed his lips with his thumb and shuffled his feet in the hay. Pa just stared into space for a long while and then he continued, "Jennie was a good woman. She done tried real hard to take care of Tut but when she found out she was gonna have a nuther baby, the wimmen took'em under thar wings, gave'em a place to lay thar haids, and cared fer'em. Jennie mitta told'em her name was – Janet. Maybe she was ashamed and embarrassed thet her old man jist up and ran off. Her actions twern't bad, she was jist scairt. Yes, Tut has a pa! Do I knoe fer shore who the pa is? No! Jennie likely would never have come home iffen it weren't fer Baby Jo. She mitta stayed thar and waited fer her old man to come home. I guess God musta been lookin' out fer Tut and Baby Jo and Jennie musta realized thet thay would be cared fer iffen she made it back to the holler. She weren't a bad person, J.D. She was jist a mite mixed up. Ya cain't be thinkin' bad thangs 'bout Jennie cause she had two thangs whut was a blessin' fer yer ma and me. Those two thangs were Tut and Baby Jo. I reckon if Tut ever had the need to look fer his pa, or his real pa needed to look fer him, we couldn't shut the door. Like ya larned frum the skunks, love ain't got no boundries! Ya don't shut the door on love. Thar's another thang I need to be a tellin' ya, J.D. Me and Grampaw knocd this day would git here. It was jist a matter of time before the two of ya would be askin' questions. Ye was too young to understand the nature of thangs when Jennie died. So, we decided to wait till ye got a little bit older to understand. When we went ta the city, me and Grampaw knoed ya would be searchin' fer answers. Grampaw and Tut ain't jist checkin' on the house. Grampaw's tellin' Tut exactly whut I been a sayin'. Don't be a fearin' 'bout the past. Iffen ya take care of today, tomorrie will tarn out jist fine."

After Pa and I sat there for awhile, the world seemed to lift off my shoulders and peace came over my very soul. I wasn't afraid anymore. I realized that Pa and Grampaw would be there for us – no matter what happened; they would be there for us.

Hand and hand, Grampaw and Tut sauntered into the barn.

Tut looked at me and said, "Ma gave me and Baby Jo a true legacy of love. A real family thet loves us!"

# A VERY SPECIAL THANKSGIVING

"I am so thankful for so many things in my life. I am truly thankful! I'm thankful for your mother, God rest her soul, and for my two daughters. I guess you know my boys were daughters!" Daddy laughed aloud. "I've done many things in my life, some good and some bad. I've experienced things that most people never have the opportunity to do and have seen many changes in this old world ... from covered wagons to men walking on the moon. However, thinking about my childhood and reflecting on the past, those were the days of wonderment and great joy."

Our house didn't have electricity, running water from a pipe, gas stoves, an in door bathroom or any of the things we so naturally take for granted. Our life was simple and love was real. Sure, I've told you about getting the daylights whacked out on my backside after doing something I shouldn't have done, but I need to set the record straight. Pa, Ma, Grammaw or Grampaw never abused any of us kids. In fact, most times when I should have been waylaid, all they did was set me down and gave me a good tongue lashing which lasted longer than a preacher hung up in a Sunday sermon did. They never put any of us kids down but impressed upon our minds a very to-the-point, oft-quoted phrase from the Bible:

"Do unto others as you would have them do unto you."

Well, back to my story–

After our trek to the city and finding out about Tut's daddy and knowing that Pa and Grampaw would take care of Tut and Baby Jo, no matter what happened, we were looking forward to a very special day: Thanksgiving.

Our neck of the woods was chock-full of game and wild turkeys. We only had wild game to eat in the winter because the animals were not foraging to build nests to procreate their species. During the springtime, Grammaw wouldn't allow us to hunt for animals. "Them lil' babies shore nuff need thar momma. Don't'cha dare be shootin' them shotguns. Yore liable to make the momma's milk go sour whilst thay be a trien to duck them flyin' pellets. Bad enough fer'em to be jerked up by somethin' wiff four laigs' or swooped up by long-winged critters wiff claws. Thay don't be a needin' two-laigged varmints poachin'em."

Since it wasn't springtime and we knew Grammaw wasn't going to read us the riot act, we headed for the woods. The day before Thanksgiving, Pa, Grampaw, Tut and I set off bright and early to get a turkey. Grampaw got his shotgun down from the mantle, loaded up his coat pocket with shells and waited until Pa did the same. Tut and I weren't allowed to tote any guns. In fact, the guns were never loaded until we reached and sat down in our favorite blind. A great motto oft quoted by Pa and Grampaw was, "Better safe than sorry!" What did Tut and I tote? Apples! I don't believe anything tasted better than munching on a red, crisp apple; sitting under a tree waiting patiently on our old turkey to come within shooting distance.

The air whistling down the draw was telling us that the winter cold would soon be here and to be on guard. Usually around Thanksgiving, the temperature in the woods would drop several degrees because the sunlight couldn't get through the treetops. Our butts were getting cold as we sat on the damp, dew-kissed leaves and the air around us would scatter with white mist as we puckered our lips and blew warm air from our mouths. It was as though we could actually see the air in front of our faces.

We sat under the tree for quite awhile before any sign of wildlife came within our view. Pa nudged Grampaw and pointed toward a big pile of brush, about twenty feet away from where we were sitting. There were big tree limbs lying on a downward slope. The limbs had apparently been there for some time, because old bushes and scrub oaks had sprouted around the area where the limbs came to rest. The newly sprouted shrubbery held the broken limbs securely to the ground. It was hard to tell, from where we were sitting, if the tree limbs had made a natural harbor for the turkeys. Old turkeys liked to gather under brush for security and warmth. Only time would tell.

A few seconds later, Pa and Grampaw gently began to stand up. Slowly, with almost precision movements, they slipped their hands into the coat pockets. They took out two shells each, cracked the barrel of the shotguns and placed the shells in the chambers. Very quietly, almost in a mime state, Pa and Grampaw brought the shotguns up toward their shoulders. They aimed precisely toward the brush. Soon, three turkeys came peeking out of the brush.

When the turkeys got about ten feet away from the brush into a partial clearing, Pa and Grampaw nodded at one another, placed their fingers on the trigger and squeezed in unison. Blam! Blam! Blam! Blam! The stillness surrounding our little corner of the world filled with thunderous, ear shattering shotgun blasts. The sound of the percussion made Tut and me start to shake. I don't know if it was from the cold or anticipated excitement for a good Thanksgiving meal.

Pa, Grampaw, Tut and I began walking toward the clearing. By golly, as I live and breathe, Pa and Grampaw had killed five turkeys with four shots. Three turkeys were lying in the clearing and two were under the brush. Pa and Grampaw looked at one another in total disbelief. They were hoping, at least, to kill one turkey for Thanksgiving. However, they managed to wipe out five turkeys – at the same time. Mouths gaping open, Pa looked at Grampaw and said, "Whut in tarnation is Ma 'n Grammaw gonna do wiff five turkeys? Thay ain't got a stove big enough or a hole in the ground fer all these here birds. We shore nuff cain't eat all these here birds!"

Grampaw said with a chuckle, "Ya best be a comin' up wiff an answer afore we git home. I ain't got a mind to be traipsin' home wiff five of these here birds! I like turkey but I shore don't like it enough to choak it down fer a full year!"

Pa took some cord from his pocket, wrapped it around the feet of each turkey, securing it with a tree branch and flung two of the turkeys over his shoulder. Grampaw took one and Tut and I took the other two. I have to tell you those turkeys were heavy.

On the way home Pa stopped dead in his tracks, turned to us and said, "I knoe whut we'll do wiff these birds! We'll give Ma and Grammaw two – one fer Thanksgivin' and put one in the smoke house fer Christmas. J. D., you and Tut git these here birds back to the house. Me and Grampaw will be home in a bit. Iffen Ma says anythin' 'bout whar we are, jist tell her we'll be home in a jiffy. Don't be a tellin' her 'bout gittin' five birds. Jist tell 'em thet me and Grampaw decided to visit over at the Newleys' place fer a spell. Ya hear?"

"Yes, sir, Pa, ya can count on us. Come on, Tut, let's be a gittin' home."

Tut and I headed off towards home. Grampaw and Pa headed in the opposite direction. When we arrived home, the girls, Ma and Grammaw were surprised when we came home proudly displaying two turkeys. Tut said, "This here turkey is fer Thanksgivin'. Pa said to git this here bird gutted fer him and he'd poke it in the smoke house fer Christmas."

Grammaw said, "I knoe thet God takes care of us in many ways. I'm jist glad ya didn't git any more turkeys. I ain't too fond of eatin' thet much turkey."

Little did she know! Trouble is, when there were just two of them to cook for, I'm sure a turkey was more than they needed. However, with five kids and four adults sitting down to a Thanksgiving meal, you could rest assured, very little would be left over to make another meal.

About two hours later, Pa and Grampaw came shuffling up the lane. All they were carrying was the shotguns. As they neared the front stoop, Pa yelled, "Fetch us the cleaning rod." They sat down on the stoop, broke open the barrel of the guns and proceeded to ram a piece of old cloth soaked with cleaning oil down the opening end of the guns. That was to clean the residue from the barrel and keep the guns in good working order.

Ma was standing at the chopping block when Pa yelled, "Hey, Ma, them's pretty good-lookin' birds, ain't thay? We shore nuff had a hard time findin' one bird. We was rite lucky to git two." Pa winked at Grampaw.

Grammaw was cleaning the big bird, which was not an easy task. Those big thick feathers stuck into the skin tighter than a corset, and jerking them out took a lot of determination. Then came the hot water dunk. Hot water usually releases any pinfeathers that stubbornly refuse to turn loose from the skin. If any pinfeathers remain on the skin, then it was time for the fire singe. Grammaw would take a real long hickory stick, ram it through the bird, hold it over the fire, turning the bird very slowly, and then plunge it into cold water. Then she would rub the turkey skin with hog lard to keep it pliable until she was prepared to cook it. She placed the big bird, rubbed heavily with freshly picked sage and hog lard, into a large iron pot, covered it with a heavy iron lid, and waited for Grampaw and Pa to lower it into a big "cooking" hole.

The cooking hole was a deep hole large enough for a big, round iron pot. It was about four feet deep and one foot wider than the pot. Grampaw would heap piles of wood inside the hole and burn them until the coals measured ten inches deep or more. Then Grampaw would slide the big pot down inside the hole. He then added additional kindling on top of the big pot, as needed. It was hard to believe buried beneath a mound of scalding hot coals was a turkey in a pot. We tended coals all night long.

Very early on Thanksgiving morning, Ma and Grammaw would get up before the chickens and begin preparing food fit for a king. They began making pies. Apple pie and buttermilk pie. Apple pie sprinkled with cinnamon and buttermilk pie smelled somewhat like lemon. Boy, that was enough to drive us nuts. The smell of pies cooking that early in the morning made a body crave food all day long. Then came the hot rolls. The aroma of yeast permeated the whole house. A mixture of bread dressing delicately entwined with sage tugged at our taste glands. Home-canned green beans and potatoes seasoned with bacon drippings were competing with all the other aromas. A pot of giblet gravy even vied for attention. It was a heavenly aromatic pleasure.

Foregoing a breakfast like the one we normally had, we all waited for the big meal. It took some doing to wait that long, but somehow, some way, we all managed.

At last, it was time to unveil the enormous turkey baking in the cooking hole. Grampaw and Pa scraped the hot coals away from the big iron lid, took two long hooked rods, placed them under the handles and lifted the big pot. The oven, hidden in the ground, was extremely hot. Since they couldn't carry the pot inside the house, Ma took a large pewter platter outside. Carefully, the turkey adorned the plate. Grampaw and Pa did the honors of carrying the big bird to the table.

That big old bird was a deep crusty brown on the outside;

moist and tender on the inside. All the wild sage and hog lard had richly flavored the meat and made the drippings into a bread sopping free-for-all. Grampaw carved the meat and generously heaped it on each of our plates: along with all the other delicious, mouth-watering trimmings.

Our house held the most wonderful atmosphere. As we all sat down to enjoy our Thanksgiving meal, each of us said a prayer. Before we could take a bite of our food, Ma said we needed bow our heads once again. She began, "Dear Lord, the Newlcy, Hawkins and Jones families dropped by to wish us a good Thanksgivin'. Thay was thankin' us fer the kindness in the gift of the turkeys, whut we're not supposed to knoe 'bout. I'm thankin' ya, Lord, fer a good carin' man and lovin' Grampaw."

This Thanksgiving was truly special. Blessings abounded in so many ways. We knew the meaning of love, were thankful for all the beautiful everyday pleasures in life, and delighted in the great joy we felt in one simple unselfish gesture – the gift of sharing.

# THE BEGINNING OF
# A GREAT CHRISTMAS

The thought of Christmas brings fond memories and caresses for the holiday season, my innermost passion. One Christmas stands out as if it was yesterday.

I am going to tell you about the season for great rejoicing and our family, especially Pa. He was known for giving great joy to many people.

People in the hollers were not wealthy, and that included us. Even though Pa had just about all the work he needed; he was never idle. When they completed all the chores around the home place, he and Grampaw would set out for the city. They didn't just go to the city for pleasure; they went there to work. At the time, I never gave it much thought. I always believed Pa and Grampaw needed to get away just like Ma and Grammaw when they went to a quilting bee or had women over at our house. Kids, at the time, were not privy to financial information or questioned adult authority.

It was about three weeks before Christmas and we were anxious about getting a Christmas tree, making ornaments and savoring the idea of tempting, mouth-watering sugar crystal popcorn.

Ma and Grammaw would combine flour and water and cook it until it was the consistency of thick gravy. The concoction would cool and we would use it as paste. All of us kids would take turns in cutting out strips of paper, usually from a newspaper from the city, curl the strips around our fingers and link them together, making a circular ring. Then we'd take the flour glue, smear it across the open ends of the rings and loop them together, making a paper chain. Before long, we would have a paper chain twenty to thirty feet long. In our eyes, it was a masterpiece and would be beautiful on our Christmas tree.

Pa would go to the woods and gather up a basket of Sweetgum balls. Ranging in colors of tan to dark brown, Sweetgum balls are beautiful when hanging tightly from a tree in the forest. When they fall on the ground it hurts the feet while trying to walk upon them. In fact, twisting an ankle while walking across them is almost a certainty. The barbs on the tips aren't for easy handling. Before we could place twine on the Sweetgum balls, Ma would spread them on an old screen, shake them very hard to get any type of bugs out of the crevices and hand us kids a ball of twine. Putting socks on our hands, we gingerly picked up one at a time and tied the twine around the little star-shaped barbs. They would look beautiful hanging on the boughs of the Christmas tree.

The same flour mixture we used for glue would be thickened with more flour and some salt. Each of us kids would get a couple of hands full and began molding differently shaped ornaments. We'd poke a hole through the dough, set them aside to dry and boast of how pretty our creations would look when we finally got our tree; but we would have to wait.

However, we did not plan one little episode with the flour mixture. It was spontaneous. The old kitchen table was long and handmade. The bench we sat upon while we ate was against the wall. It had a long loose plank placed over two supports. Pa never nailed it down the plank. The plank was replaced with a longer, sturdier board as we grew. When the plank became dirty, Ma wanted to be able to take the plank outside and scrub it thoroughly.

Well, Ma had taken the plank off the supports and laid it at an angle across the table. To cool the mixture, when she finished cooking it, she placed the pot of goop on the edge of the loose plank. Tut came bouncing into the kitchen, not paying attention to what he was doing, started to sit down on the plank, which was not there, lost his balance, and his elbows hit the edge of the loose plank. All of a sudden, the pot of goop, at the opposite end of the plank went flying into the air straight for Tut. We watched the pot sail through the air, turn upside down and land square dab on top of his head. Splat!

Flour goop started oozing down his face and neck and down the front of his shirt. Grammaw ran to Tut as quickly as she could and began trying to lift the pot of goopy glue off his head. The pot was stuck to Tut's head like stick tights on a pair of nylon socks. Grammaw, with all her might, tugged and pulled at that pot. All the pot did was gurgle and burp. We all were in a state of panic because we thought the goopy glue was still hot. When we realized Tut was not in danger of being burned but merely glued and matted together, we all began to laugh. Poor Tut just sat there.

When Grammaw finally got the pot off Tut's head, all you could see was his eyes. Ma grabbed a long wooden spoon and began scraping glue from the top of his head. She tried to wash his face. The more she washed, the more the glue ran. His shirt was caked with the glue drippings and the table and floor were slicker than goose grease.

Somehow, Tut managed to unbutton the top two buttons and jerked it over his head. He handed the shirt to Ma and she washed the shirt the best she could and hung it on the clothesline to dry. As Ma hung the shirt on the clothesline, she pressed the sleeves sideways. It looked like someone was stretching out their arms, waiting for a long lost friend. When that shirt finally dried, it was stiffer than a board.

After that little fiasco and making another pot of glue, we finished making our flour ornaments.

There wasn't much we couldn't find to decorate our tree.

The woods were abundant with red berries, vines to make wreaths, pinecones, silk-pods, water lily blossoms that we called rattle pins, hedge apples (commonly called horse apples), cattails, and a vast variety of other things grown by nature. Our Christmas tree might not have the brightly colored glass balls so beautifully adorning houses of grandeur, but to us, it was impressive and a natural thing of beauty.

Then came the popcorn. Ma would take chunk of hog lard, place it in an old iron pot, add popcorn kernels, and shake the pot until the kernels began to swell and pop. Since all of us kids were so anxious to begin stringing the white popcorn, we hovered over the stove waiting for the first batch to finish popping. Grammaw would hand each of us a pail of corn, some needles and thread and we would sit in front of the fireplace: stringing and eating popcorn. It would take a while to string a garland because popcorn breaks, fingers get jabbed with needle pricks, and soon one of us would complain. Being in a stooped position for such a long time made our backs ache. It was a minor inconvenience, especially when we saw the garland draped over the branches.

At long last, it was time to get our tree. We were exuberant with jittery excitement and watched as Pa got the axe and an old makeshift sled. The sled had a rope handle to haul our Christmas tree back to the house.

This was a family affair, so we bundled up in warm clothes and headed for the 'deep' woods. We plodded up past Grammaw and Grampaw's old house and past the cemetery where Jennie lay. We came to a small clearing. North of the clearing was a grove of cedar trees. It seemed like we walked for miles hunting just the right tree. We passed up several cedars because they were as large as our front room, seedlings no bigger than a bird's leg and scraggly ones eaten by cedar moths. Grampaw yelled out for us, "By gum, I done found the tree. Fetch the axe and give me a hand."

There it was! It was as tall as Grampaw and didn't have an empty branch. Pa told us kids to stand back as he began to chop down the tree. Before we knew it, they had loaded the tree on the sled and we headed home. Just minutes before we reached the warm house, Pa shinnied up an old elm tree and retrieved an arm full of mistletoe.

During the wintertime, mistletoe is a fungus that grows on trees that lose their leaves. It forms from the deposits of bird droppings. Usually, you can see mistletoe growing the hard, yellowish green leaves and stems during the summer and then when it gets cold the little white berries pop forth and send the signal for picking.

It is a beautiful sight when all the trees have lost their leaves. The trees standing stark naked against the backdrop of a winter mist and hazy skies is sheer grandeur. I always thought it was nature's way of trying to keep them warm; displaying the outline of an endless array of trees mingled with the cedars and pines so elegantly perched with needled branches. It was a masterpiece; painted by God for our landscape.

While we were warming by the fireplace, Pa and Grampaw took the tree to the barn, sawed the tree trunk flat and nailed it to a wooden base. When they brought it into house, all of us kids raced to begin decorating. While we were placing each ornament on the tree, Pa was arranging the mistletoe over each door and yelling for Ma to come see the special affects. Then when Ma got under one of the branches, Pa would reach out and give her a big kiss. It would make Ma's cheeks blush bright red, but somehow we knew Ma loved getting kisses from Pa. While they were hugging and kissing, Grammaw was in the kitchen fending off Grampaw's advances of kisses. When Pa and Grampaw decided they had embarrassed Ma and Grammaw, they went about their chores.

I could hear Grammaw tell Ma, "I jist love thet old codger to daith." Then they went about making a special treat. Sugar-coated popcorn for us to eat and ginger cookies to hang on the Christmas tree.

Grammaw would take sugar, water, salt and vanilla, boil it until it crystallized and then, in a fine stream, gently drizzle it over the popped corn. It tasted so delicious as the sweet sugar would melt with the lightly salted popcorn. It was fit for a king.

As we hung the last strand of popcorn around the tree, Pa said, "I reckon this here old tree jist mite be the purtiest thang in the holler, but it shore nuff needs a topper. I reckon I jist mite have the proper thang to set it off. Iffen you kids'll traipse over here and close yore eyes real tight, we jist mite be able to find somethin' rite purty."

We all gathered around Pa with our eyes shut and waited. Pa said, "Ye can open'em up now." Pa was holding the most beautiful silver paper star we had ever seen. Pa walked over to the tree, placed the star upon the top and said, "Iffen a star is good enough fer the beginnin' of baby Jesus, I reckon this here lil' star is good enough fer us."

Pa was right. It was the beginning of a very special Christmas.

# A CHRISTMAS TO REMEMBER

After we had decorated our beautiful Christmas tree, all we had to do was wait on Christmas. It seemed like the next three weeks would drag on forever. For some crazy reason, when you're a kid, the days seem to slowly creep along. As a person ages, and grows into adulthood, the days fly past all too quickly. These days, I go to sleep in January and wake up in December.

Christmas around our house was a most enjoyable time. Because it was so cold outside, our only entertainment was to play checkers and dominoes. Occasionally, Ma would let the girls use the scissors to cut out paper dolls and Tut and I would draw pictures.

Most of the time, we would curl up close to the fireplace and listen to Grammaw. She would tell stories about her childhood. We thought we had it hard! Shoot, our chores were mild compared to all the things she went through. Some very hard and tedious routines fell upon her shoulders. We could sit for hours listening to the same stories. They were special exciting events, and every time she told them she would add something extra. If it got to the point of sheer boredom, Ma would let each of us take turns making some kind of goodie. We might make gingerbread, sorghum molasses cookies or bread pudding. Let me tell you, food back then sure tasted good and stuck to your rib cage!

None of us kids expected much for Christmas. Ma always said, "Iffen ya don't expect the world, ye ain't gonna ever be unhappy. Iffen ye git a little bit, be thankful. Iffen ye git a lot, thank the good Lord." I don't think we were ever unhappy, or if we were, it never showed. Happiness to us was a mud puddle and a clod of dirt.

The week before Christmas was as cold as a witch's broom and the atmosphere was heavy with moisture. It appeared that snow was looming on the horizon. Pa and Grampaw had hitched up the wagon and set off for the city and wouldn't be home for the biggest part of the day. I had visions of them being caught in a snowstorm or having to stay in the city, unable to return home. It wouldn't be Christmas without Pa or Grampaw, because they always told Bible stories. Our favorite story was about the Magi following the star in search of the newborn King.

I guess it was about the time we got ready for bed when Pa and Grampaw came home. Tut and I had gone to bed in the loft and were having a hard time trying to fall asleep. As the wind whistled outside, we sank beneath the covers. Before I went to sleep, I thought I could hear Ma, Pa, Grammaw, and Grampaw. They were talking and sitting at the kitchen table drinking coffee as the kerosene lantern flickered and cast long tall shadows against the wall.

"Did'ya have airy luck findin' whut we needed, Pa?"

"Shore did, Hon. I stuck'em in the barn. First light, I'll fetch'em. Me and Grampaw'll take the kids fer a buggy ride whilst ye and Grammaw git to werk fixin'em."

"Whut about the other thangs? Er thay whar ya figgered to poke'm? Grammaw whispered.

"Don't'cha be worrin' yore purty lil' haid, Grammaw. We done tucked'em away fer safe keepin'. I reckon thay'll be jist fine," Grampaw replied.

I'm not sure how long they talked but I knew they were up to something, or maybe I was dreaming.

The next morning we awoke to a light dusting of snow. Tut

and I helped Pa and Grampaw load two ricks of wood on the stoop near the backdoor and covered them with hay and corn shucks to keep them dry from snow. If the wood got wet, it would take longer for them to burn. We had a woodshed full of dry wood, but Pa always made it easier for Ma and Grammaw. All they had to do was reach out the door and grab what they needed.

When we finished having our breakfast, Pa looked at Grampaw and said, "Fetch the buggy. I reckon we jist mite take a ride. How 'bout goin' up over the ridge fer a spell. Ma, Grammaw, ya best be a gittin' on yer coats and bundle up rite good."

Ma said, "Pa, we figger ta stay home. It'll be good fer the kids, tho. Ya'll jist be careful. Be shore to yell when ya start back up the lane. Me and Grammaw will fix ya somethin' hot to drink. Don't'cha fergit to yell!"

Somehow, I knew they wouldn't be going on this buggy ride. I wasn't dreaming! I did hear them talking last night.

We were gone all day long. Grampaw drove that buggy around in circles. Our butts were getting sore from sitting and nearly frozen solid. If it hadn't been for the blankets piled around our bodies, it would have taken us a week to thaw. If anyone accidentally hit our noses, they would have fallen into our laps. We sure weren't hungry! We had plenty to eat, because Ma had prepared a basket of food for us to munch on. She knew we would be gone for the bigger part of the day. In my way of thinking, they could have told us to go play in the barn. At least we would have been out of the elements.

As we turned down the lane and approached the house, Pa and Grampaw began yelling. They were screaming to the top of their lungs. The way the wind was blowing, everyone within five miles could hear them. All of us kids just looked at one another and glanced at Pa and Grampaw out the corner of our eyes. We thought they had lost it. Their yelling spooked the hell out of the horses and we tore through the yard at full speed. We didn't even stop at the front door. Those dad-blamed horses didn't stop till they reached the barn. It was bad enough to have our bodies colder than kraut but standing up to walk on feet that felt like nubs – well, it was like walking on stilts.

We managed to hobble up to the house and, in unison, collapsed in front of the fireplace. Every time we tried to move, it felt like little tiny needles sticking into our skin. I swore, right there and then, if they wanted to go on a buggy ride in ten-degree weather with air swishing through their ears and freezing the hair in the nose, I was going to stay home. Yes siree, they could just count me out of their harebrained, lollipaloozer schemes!

Finally, it was Christmas Eve. Grammaw had hung beautifully decorated homemade stockings on the mantle and told us kids not to touch them because Saint Nick or Santa Claus, as most people called him, would be looking down the chimney to see how many kids lived here. He would only stop his reindeer if he saw any stockings.

I thought that was pretty stupid and said, "Jist how can he see down thet chimley? Thay ain't no way fer him to peer through the smoke a billowin' up thet chimley. Jist who is thet Saint Nick? Why don't he jist nok on the door. Grammaw! Why, yore jist pullin' 'er laigs! Why, thay ain't no Saint Nick and thay ain't no Santie Claus."

Grammaw laughed and said, "I'm a tellin' ya thet Saint Nick knoes everthang 'bout ya. He's got this here book thet he totes and iffen ya ain't been good, ya git a blak mark run through yer name. I done seen him. Iffen ya don't be thinkin' I knoe whut I'm talkin' 'bout, ya jist wait and see. He wears a fancy red fandangled suit and brings the presents fer lil' kids."

All of us kids were listening intently to Grammaw. We sat there, glued to every word that came out of her mouth. She spoke with such great information about Saint Nick or Santa

Claus that before she was finished, Tut and I was sure of one thing. If he did have a black book, knew every bad deed we did, could see down chimneys, had flying reindeer and knew where we lived and left presents for kids ... well, we could kiss any thought of Christmas presents good-bye!

It was beginning to get dark outside and Pa said, "Grampaw, ya knoe whut we fergot ta do? We plum fergot to check on Mr. Jones over past the holler. He was feelin' rite poorley. Shore nuff cain't break thet promise to check on him and his missus. Reckon we best set out fer a spell. Ma, do ya got sumthin' hot fer'em to eat?"

Ma fixed a basket of food and handed it to Pa. He and Grampaw set out on a trek to the Jones house. In my heart, I just knew that our Christmas wouldn't be the same without Pa and Grampaw. They wouldn't be here to tell us Bible stories. I know, the way I was feeling was selfish, but I wanted them to be home with us.

It was getting later and later, and no sign of Pa or Grampaw. Effie Mae and Aunt Sukie were making sure the secret Christmas presents were still inside the Christmas tree branches. They were special gifts for Grammaw, Grampaw, Ma and Pa. They had taken one of Grammaw's real old dresses that normally would be used for rags, cut off the pretty lace, made squares of the material and sewed them into spice bags. They stuffed them with lavender flowers and dried spices.

Tut and I carved hearts from some old wooden pine chunks, poked a hole at the top and put a long piece of twine through the hole. We thought those little carved hearts would look so pretty hanging around Ma and Grammaw's necks. We also whittled two long-handled wooden spoons from oak: for Ma and Grammaw. They weren't perfect, but when you don't have any money to spend, a handmade present given with love and from the heart sure makes you feel good.

For Pa and Grampaw, all of us kids worked together and

made pipe stands, a fiddle and banjo holder and, believe it or not, a small broom to sweep up the fireplace ashes. We used every kind of softwood we could find for the stands and holders. Grampaw always made whittling look as easy, but we had a very hard time getting that wood to cooperate. We made the broom from very fine willow branches and corn fronds. It took us a long time to shred the corn fronds and even longer to tie them onto a wooden stick. We worked on the broom for weeks and laughed when Aunt Sukie said, "Iffen thay git this thang stuck in the hot coals, it's liable to burn up afore thay stomp it out."

Right before we decided to go to bed, a loud thud hit the front stoop. It sounded like one of the supports holding the roof broke and fell. All of a sudden, you could hear the front door shake. Someone was pounding on it so hard that it rattled the pane glass window. The first thing that entered my mind was Pa and Grampaw.

Ma and Grammaw stood at the door with all of us kids hanging on their backsides. Nobody ever pounded on a door that hard unless someone had died or was badly hurt. As Ma opened the door, we gasped! There he stood: as big as life. A big, red-suited Santa Claus. He was tall with a round belly and a white beard hung down to his waist. His hat was red like his suit except for the white fluffy cotton around the brow. A ball of cotton hung from the tip of his hat and shook when he said, "Ho, Ho, Ho! Merry Christmas!"

Baby Jo began to cry and hid under the bed. The rest of us kids stood there in shock. Grammaw was telling the truth. There was a Saint Nick! Santa Claus reached around his back, jerked a big heavy sack hanging from his shoulders and plopped it down on the porch.

"I betcha thar's sumthin' fer ya. Lookie here." He pulled out two bags of marbles, five pair of brand-new gloves, and some store-bought paper dolls. We could hardly believe our eyes.

Before we could say a word or thank him for our presents he said, "This is fer the believers, jest to let ya knoe that Santie Claus is fer real. Ya best git to bed afore Christmas day gits here. Santie's got a passel to do." He turned around and before we knew it, he just disappeared into the night.

We were so excited and full of awe at the sight of Santie Claus that we weren't even aware Pa and Grampaw were standing in the kitchen.

As we caught the glimpse of them standing there, we hollered, "Pa, Grampaw, did'ja see'em? It was Santie Claus! Lookie here, see whut he brung us. He done brung us sum real warm gloves, doogies fer Tut and me, and paper dolls fer the girls. Boy oh boy, Pa, this here Christmas shore is a gooder'n."

Ma and Grammaw were smiling and Pa and Grampaw reached out and hugged us all. Grampaw had tears welling up in his eyes and said in a breaking voice, "Well, Christmas ain't here yet. Ya best be gittin' sum shuteye. Tomorrie jist mite hold surprises fer us all."

Reluctantly, we went to bed. It was more than we could stand. The sight of a real Santa Claus standing in our doorway sent shivers up our spines. Because we had been out in the cold all day, bumping and bouncing around in the buggy, it didn't take us long to fall asleep. We laid the marbles and gloves beside us to make sure they were there when we woke up.

When we woke up the next morning, a sight to beat all sights was right there, beneath our tree. There was a big red wagon with rubber wheels, two French harps, three baby dolls, a treadle sewing machine, two bolts of material and brand-new store-bought shoes. We couldn't believe our eyes and didn't know what to look at first.

Ma said, "I reckon Santie Claus fergot to leave this stuff. He must'a come back whilst we were asleep. Jist have fun. Me 'n Grammaw's gonna fix a powerful good Christmas meal."

It was almost noon. The front yard began to fill with all our neighbors. The children and grown-ups were crowded around and in our house. The women had brought food and were hugging Pa and Grampaw, telling them how much they appreciated everything. They were buzzing about Santa Claus visiting their houses and how the faces of their youngsters had lighted up as they received precious gifts. Gifts their children wouldn't have had without the kind and generous giving Santa Claus.

Stranger still were the different descriptions of Santa Claus. Several people saw him as tall and big-bellied and others described him as being shorter and fat-bellied. It amazed all of us kids as we told about what we saw. What we couldn't understand was how Santa Claus managed to be at different places at the same time. It was a mystery to us how he could find us all in the dark, knew how many kids lived in each house and what our secret heart's desire was.

Every one of us kids played outside. We felt so warm inside that we didn't even feel the cold. We took turns pulling each other in the red wagon and played games. The boys were playing doogies, mumblypeg, and having races while all the girls were playing with their new baby dolls or new tea sets.

Hidden inside my pocket was my most precious gift: a beautiful silver and wooden French harp. Every now and then, I would sneak it out of my pocket and blow it, trying to figure out if I was to blow air inside it or suck out the air. Both ways made wonderful musical tones. One way or another, I would eventually learn to play the French harp.

Christmas day was heavenly. Everyone was happy, cheerful and full of love. We shared a big meal with all the hill folk – no turkey! We had ham and all the fixings that were lovingly prepared by Ma and Grammaw. The women folk, from neighboring homes, brought vinegar pies – yes, I said vinegar pies – and great vanilla taffy. It was as though no one wanted to go home. I knew how much the hill folk loved and admired

## WINDY JOHN'S RAINBOW AND THE POT O' GOLD

Pa and Grampaw for their generous nature, and Ma and Grammaw in their willingness to always be there in time of need, but this day was different. It was full of Godly love.

Everyone loved his or her presents. Ma and Grammaw wore the heart necklaces with pride and used the wooden spoons for as long as I can remember. The girls beamed with joy as they watched Ma and Grammaw tenderly caress and sniff the sachet holders as they placed them with great care around the house. Pa and Grampaw delighted in the wooden pipe holder and fiddle stands. They cautiously used the broom. That old broom held together for many ash sweepings.

As for me, well – this Christmas was the most blessed Christmas of my childhood. It would be many years later before I found out exactly how or why, Pa and Grampaw was loved by so many people and how Santa Claus managed to be so tall and short and make so many people happy. But that's my secret!

All I will say is: thank you, God, for my Pa and Grampaw's unselfish gestures and for Ma and Grammaw's ability to sew.

This was truly a Christmas to remember!

# A WINTER'S WRATH

It was so cold outside. The bitter wind would cut through the valley as though it was searching for some place to get warm. Normally, most of us in the hollers didn't anticipate a bad winter. We just considered it as an inconvenient seasonal change. The only thing we didn't enjoy? Being cooped up in the house with nothing to do but pester one another. We still had our chores to do, like checking on the critters or hauling wood from the woodshed, but those were typical things a person did when you lived in the country. This season, though, was not the normal routine.

All summer and most of the fall season, you could see changes in how the critters were acting and the bark of the trees seemed to tighten and thicken around trunks of trees and branches. The sky would light up with a beautiful glow around the treetops and then vanish into a dark, low-lying veil of clouds. We knew something had to be looming on the horizon but weren't sure exactly what it was. Grammaw and Grampaw's wise words of wisdom always said that if we had fog in the summer, we could expect a hard winter.

Being a kid and hearing all the folklore from Grampaw and Grammaw about the moon and stars and the balance it made on the earth made us wonder if they were right. Grammaw would always say, "The changes in the moon dictates everthang whut comes our way." I know they planted crops by the light of the moon. Not literally! They didn't go out at midnight and plant seed. They used the phases of the moon to know when to plant underground and topside crops. I truly believe that's why we always had an abundance of good food.

It was late summer day, and I remember Tut and I wanted to go fishing. We had dug for worms until we were sick of worms. We couldn't find one single worm, even though we had dug holes all over the pasture. We even resorted to pounding the soil with rocks. Usually, pounding the soil will bring the worms up from the deep cool soil, but no such luck. The soil was unusually hard from the lack of rain, so we gave up trying to find fishing worms.

We found a few crickets and grasshoppers, but the fish were deep in the water. By the time we got the crickets and grasshoppers on our lines and plopped them into the water, they would fall off the hooks. We could never get them down deep enough in the water to tempt the fish. We decided to forget about fishing until Tut, lying down on the creek bank, looked up in one of the big Catalpa trees and spied a mess of wooly worms. Tut shimmied up the tree and began dropping them one by one until we had at least fifty, big old black and orange, wirehaired wooly worms. Some of them were as long as our index finger, but all they were was hair. We couldn't even poke the hook into their skinny little bellies. We gave up the notion of fishing and took the remaining wooly worms back to the house.

When Grammaw saw what we had, her words were, "It's a bad sign! Ya cain't be a loafin' jist rite now. Best be a loadin' up th' wood box, git th' hay in th' barn, 'n make shore th' chicken house roof ain't got no holes. I reckon we done been showed whut the winter is a bringin'. Go show them werms ta yer grampaw and yer pa."

They took one look at those wooly worms and laid down a plan of action. Each one of us, with the exception of Baby Jo and someone taking turns watching her would have to make hay while the sun was shining. The wood shed would need stocking with a surplus of wood. The stoop at the back porch would have to be fully loaded with wood, all the hay in the pasture would need to be hauled to the south side of the barn, and any cracks or holes between the chinked logs would have to be filled with clay mud or anything handy to keep out the cold weather. We completed all the chores and hoped the weather wouldn't be as severe as the signs indicated.

Most winters would bring a light dusting of snow and maybe if we were lucky, we'd have enough snowfall to build a snowman or make snow ice cream. We just didn't dream that this particular winter would be so bad!

As I said, the wind was biting and howled for several days. The temperature dipped so low that walking on the grass felt as though we were walking on spike-tipped shoes. Every step would mash the grass and leave footprints embedded on the hardened soil. After awhile, the fog that crept into the valley shrouded the surroundings with an icy, lacy appearance. Each tree branch, encrusted with a thin layer of glistening frozen water crystals, looked like millions of shimmering diamonds. It was an absolutely beautiful sight.

Then without warning, rain began to fall. We could hear the raindrops hitting the tin roof on the wood shed. Rain hitting a tin roof has a calming effect and makes bodies want to sink into a deep slumber or snuggle very close with someone you love. It's like warming the body with hot cups of sassafras tea.... A real soothing effect.

Then the rain changed to thunderous sleet. It pelted the tin roof so hard and with such force that we could actually feel the noise. It was deafening.

The fireplace and old black-bellied stoves cranked up with generous heat, toasted our backsides until we felt warm enough to turn around and cook the other side. Fireplace heat is addictive! A body just can't get enough warmth, and no fireplace is ever big enough to accommodate several persons standing side to side, all at one time.

Having to go to bed when it was so cold outside wasn't hard to do, except when you sleep in a loft. Tut and I would roast our bodies until they glowed in the dark and then make a mad dash to the ladder to get in bed before they cooled off. Although heat rises, it was like crawling into a deep freeze. The bedclothes were so cold that Ma had to take some big rocks, heat them on the cook stove, wrap them in old cloths and then shove them down toward our feet. While the feet were warm, the rest of the body would relax. I bet we didn't move more than once the entire night.

The next morning was a shock! Because we went to bed with the chickens and woke up with the roosters, it was still somewhat dark outside. It didn't take anyone of us very long to realize just what the temperature, rain and sleet had created.

Since the old black-bellied cook stove had been stoked throughout the night with kindling placed in the kitchen, all Ma or Grammaw had to do was open the backdoor, lift whatever big pieces of wood they needed and fire up the cook stove. Grammaw reached over to open the door and it would not budge. She shoved so hard her feet slid out from under her, her legs sprawled open and she wound up on the floor, straddling the preparing table. Grammaw was faunching at the bit and giving the door old billy ned. She was fit to be tied.

Now Grammaw was not one to mince words. She yelled, "Grampaw, git yore butt in here! Ya see this here damned old door? I reckon to tell ya, thet iffen yore belly is a hankerin' fer vittles, ya best figger me a way to tote the wood offen the stoop. The door done froze shut. I done plastered my butt to the floor and I ain't aimin' to do it a secont time."

Grampaw, snickering through his old long beard, said, "Grammaw, don't be a gittin' yore drawers inna a dither. I'll jist mosey 'round the back and fetch the wood. Jist don't git yer pinfeathers ruffled. I'll be back inna a jiffy."

Pa told Grampaw that he would help him. They put on their coats and headed out the front door. They opened the door but were unprepared for what came next. Grampaw wasn't paying attention to anything. He began to walk across the front stoop in his general manner of walking, hit ice with his right foot and began skiing toward the porch support. Pa hollered for Grampaw to be careful, but it was too late. Grampaw hit that support with a thud. He wrapped around that post like a candy wrapper. Grampaw was trying to get a good grip around the support, but it was futile. The support was coated with so much ice that by the time he knew what hit him, his butt hit the ground and he began sliding, lickity split, toward the clothesline post. A very sensitive portion of his anatomy struck the clothesline post. All Grampaw could say was, "Hell's bells, I'm seein' stars! Sumthin' done broke off!"

Pa was trying very hard not to laugh because he knew the pain Grampaw was experiencing. Very cautiously, Pa began to approach Grampaw with the thoughts of extracting him from the clothesline post, but it was in vain. As Pa reached down to grab under Grampaw's armpits to lift him from the ice, Pa lost his balance and rammed Grampaw further into the post.

By this time, Grampaw was yelling to the top of his lungs. "Git offen me! I ain't got a mind to have ya frozen to my backside. Cain't ya tell thet sumthin' I got done mashed toward my innards? Er ya trien to shove it inta my haid?"

While all of this was going on, we were peering through the window, watching every bit of the slapstick comedy and finding the precarious ice escapades hilariously funny. Grammaw was hobbling around with a sore butt, and Grampaw would have one to match.

As we continued to look out the window, we were astounded. Ice was everywhere. All the majestic stately oak, elm and hickory trees were bent and shattered from the weight of the ice. Shards of tree limbs plunged to the ground and some smaller trees bent over into an arch. Our beautiful pine and cedar trees lining the edge of Frog Holler were splintered. The tops of the trees were dangling toward the earth as large tree limbs laden with the heavy ice fell through the trees like tipped-over dominoes. The frozen ice was like a silent tomb, encasing every inch of the valley and surrounding hollers. It was eerie! It looked like an ice castle and almost made the heart stop with its silent, breathtaking beauty.

All of a sudden, the silence resounded with a loud continuing crash. Since we couldn't get out the backdoor and were at the mercy of an icy foothold, we had to wait until Pa or Grampaw could get to the back of the house to check on the loud noise. We were in a dither! Go out the front door and break your neck or stay in the house and let it fall on you. One way or the other, the ice had us in its grip and controlled our every move.

Tut and I decided to go help Pa and Grampaw. We pulled on our boots, donned our hats and coats and with the aid of a fireplace poker, set out to examine the ice-covered stomping grounds. The ground, covered in small, round ice pellets made walking upright not an easy task.

Somehow, we managed to get Pa and Grampaw in an upright position, clasp each other's hands and walk very slowly by ramming the poker into the ice.

As we rounded the back stoop, a major problem confronted us. One of the large trees on the slope of Frog Holler had uprooted and was sliding down the mountain, taking out every ice-covered tree in its wake. Lucky for us, the outbuildings weren't close to the path of the tree fall. Then, without warning, the hollers began to echo with the sounds of trees splitting and tree limbs cracking. It sounded like shotgun blasts and rifle shots. The eerie silence reverberated with pops and cracks.

While Grampaw and Pa worked to free the ice-covered backdoor, Tut and I loaded our arms with firewood and headed to the front door. One by one, we had to roll each piece of firewood to the door. The girls would pick up the wood and then stack it near the fireplace. Grammaw was finally happy. She and Ma could get our breakfast started. Shoot, all Grammaw wanted was coffee. She needed that first cup of coffee to get her insides to kick in!

What came next? The outhouse. That oft-needed building far away from the house, embedded with thick ice, would be Grammaw's greatest obstacle. Or would it?

While Pa and Grampaw were sitting around trying to figure out how to get to the barn without breaking their necks, Grammaw was doing the same. Only, she didn't want to go to the barn. She needed to go to the outhouse. We could see Grammaw take deep breaths and begin pacing the floor. We knew without a shadow of a doubt Grammaw better figure out something quick or risk losing her dignity.

She reached inside the pantry, took out two good-sized copper cook pots, grabbed up two long-handled poultry forks and proceeded with her little jaunt. Grammaw was nobody's dummy. Getting off the back stoop was the easier part. She took logs, laid them in a row, sat down on them and scooted across the porch like a pro. Before she placed her feet on the icy ground, she plopped the copper cook pots side by side. Then, very slowly, she placed a knee inside each pot. Using the forks as a spike, she'd jab the forks into the ice and pull her body forward. Grammaw was in motion and we were in shock.

We watched in amazement as Grammaw reached the outhouse. She angled her body sideways, lifted one leg at a time and stuck her feet inside the pots. Then with a good hard whack, knocking the icy latch free, opened the door and went inside. Grammaw's motto, "Iffen thar's a will, thar's a way!"

When Grammaw came back to the house, she handed the pots to Pa and Grampaw and said with a smirk, "I ain't no shrinkin' violet. Ya best be a checkin' the barn."

Pa and Grampaw knew that Grammaw had outwitted them. Pa volunteered to go to the barn because Grampaw was still reeling from the aftermath of the encounter with the clothesline post. After a few maneuvers with the pots and forks, Pa reached the barn and waved that everything was ok. However, he got smart. He took the sled we used to haul our Christmas tree, placed some hay on it and used it like a scooter. Every few feet, Pa would lay the hay down, go back for more and continued this process until he made a path from every outbuilding to the house. Now the ice storm wouldn't be able to keep us cooped up in the house.

Just as we were beginning to get control of doing things, that is, being able to go to the outhouse and checking on the critters, it began to snow. All of Pa's ingenuity was covered by five inches of wet snow. The hay covered over with snow in less than twenty-four hours. At least the snow was easier to walk on but still hampered our ability to maneuver. There was only one thing to do.

Under normal circumstances, Pa would never resort to burning anything outdoors because of the danger. It would have been a disaster. One flick of a burning ember could have ignited the forest and placed everyone living in the hollers inside a timber box. But since everything was totally iced over and snow blanketed the ice, there would be no danger.

We gathered fallen branches and piled them into small heaps scattered about on our usual walkways. It took a little while to entice the wood to burn, but with a little help from dried corn shucks and kindling wood, the heaps of wet wood began to smolder. That did the trick! The snow and ice began to melt quite rapidly. We could go about our normal routines without sliding or falling.

Although the ice and snow remained on the ground for several days, we endured one of the hardest winters I can ever remember. Grampaw, having to walk very gingerly for several days, did recover from his bruised lower anatomy and swelled private parts. Grammaw's backside was black and blue for several days. Pa swore he would never again be caught hugging the backside of Grampaw.

Smart old Grammaw and good old Pa. This ice and snowstorm didn't keep us in the house, nor did it prevent us from having fun. Although the storm was debilitating to the forest and created extreme pressures in our uncomplicated little world, we managed to survive. In fact, I do believe it made us stronger.

One thing I learned from Grammaw's wise words of wisdom. "Iffen thar's a will, thar's a way and don't fergit to check them wooly werms!"

# PONCHO, RUN – IT'S CHESTER AND THE MITTIE MITES

The adults in our house were true believers in keeping things clean. The house was always spotless, the yard had to be kept raked, the barn had everything in its place, the smoke house was never out of kilter, the woodshed was neatly arranged and even the outhouse was properly maintained.

Living on the farm, there was always something to do. I believe the most unsettling, nerve-wracking thing on the farm was cleaning out the chicken house. The only reason we had a chicken house was because the chickens, having the run of the yard, was notorious for laying eggs wherever they had a mind to squat. Ma and Grammaw got tired of searching high and low for eggs to gather and didn't enjoy stepping into chicken poo on the front stoop or having chickens leap off the roof of the smoke house. Pa and Grampaw built the chicken house, enclosed by a picket fence to appease the two of them. Somehow, cleaning the chicken house always fell on Tut and me. The reason? Well, in our feeble minds, it probably kept us from pulling pranks. The amount of time-consuming trouble it always caused inflicted a great distaste of the occupants with feathers.

Once a year, usually in the hottest part of the summer, Pa would declare and wage war on anything that began to have an unsavory odor.

That meant taking clean hay, several buckets of water, lye soap, rags, a scrub brush, broom and elbow grease to every square inch of wood in the chicken house. Cleaning the chicken house took nearly all day long. That alone wasn't so bad, but it entailed more than a body could bear. It wasn't just a chicken house: it was a battle house! Let me explain.

The first thing we had to do was stack hay outside the pen. We stacked it high enough to be able to reach over the chicken fence and grab what we needed and then run like hell back into the chicken house. If the haystack got too low, we'd have to open the gate and carry in what we needed. That is, if we could dodge the low-flying, feathered, twin engine, self-propelled skin gouging wing flappers. Hopefully, we wouldn't have to open the gate too many times.

Opening the fence gate was also an invitation for feathers to escape and merely prolonged the torturous ordeal of cleaning. Those dumb chickens felt the urge to dash through the gate and then the race was on. Trying to catch forty chickens in short-winged flights, plus listening to squalks and clucks with every lunge to snatch them or crawling through grass, made us pretty cock-eyed cantankerous. Opening the gate not only released the hens. It released Poncho, the blood blistering, wild-eyed goose, and Run It's Chester, the long-spurred rooster!

Poncho was the meanest damned old goose that ever lived. Grammaw raised the gosling from the time it hatched. In fact, one year before Grammaw moved from the mountain, she found a single goose egg, lying close to the cow pond. She cradled it near her cook stove and provided the warmth it needed to hatch. When the gosling hatched, it thought Grammaw was its mother. That goose grew faster than a festered boil on the backside and had a temperament to match. Somehow, I do believe Grammaw transferred her temperament to the goose.

He was rotten to the core and worse than a pit bull. Grammaw never had the need for a watchdog. Poncho was the watchdog. He would hide behind shrubs, trees or under the stoop until a body was within a close proximity, raise up his long gray neck, make a sinister hiss, lower his head, flap his wings and run on massive webbed feet with the power of a mad dog. All of a sudden, you were on the receiving end of Poncho's long, snapping tweezerd beak. He would nip the skin until it was black and blue. He could generate blood blisters the size of a hammered thumbnail.

Run It's Chester happened to be the cock of the walk. He did not get his name from being a loveable daddy to the baby chicks! His real name was Chester, because he would pound his chest with his wings when he felt threatened. His nature was purely nasty and he could exude sweat from a cactus. I don't know what it was about me, Tut and Run It's Chester, but when we were together, it was a free-for-all. We tried everything – whistling, humming, coughing and even sneaking into the chicken house while looking very cautiously over our shoulders but Run It's Chester knew instinctively when we approached their domain. He would prance, strut and dare you to take one step through the gate.

Once inside, you took your life into your own hands. He would lower his head, scratch the ground and before you could snap your fingers, be attached to a leg with his long talon. He would flog the lower extremities with such a blow that all you could do was scream bloody murder and yell, "Run, it's Chester!" That's how he got his name: Run It's Chester.

Anyway, we had gotten all of our things together and prepared to open the gate. There stood Run It's Chester and Poncho watching our every move. Tut got behind me and I placed the buckets of water in front of my feet. Since the rooster and goose were watching the buckets, we backed up very slowly toward the chicken house door. With each backward step we took, I would inch the buckets of water backwards until we reached the door. If need be, I would have beaned and plastered old Run It's Chester and Poncho with those buckets of water. Finally, Tut unlatched the hook and we went inside.

Ye Gods! We went from one mess to another. Lucky for us the hens were already out of the roost, but the worse was yet to come.

The chicken house had forty small roosts or little cubicles for each hen. The rows of cubicles were all on one side with a narrow walkway in the front. This way you could get the eggs from the nests with very little difficulty. On the front side of the house were several tiny slats for ventilation, and one window, large enough to toss out the soiled hay and yuk from the nests. At the base of the door was a small square opening for the chickens to enter and exit. I'm here to tell you those vents and window needed to be the size of the whole state of Arkansas! It stunk to high heaven.

If you've never been in a chicken house, you don't know what you've been missing. Being in such close quarters with small vents, the door shut because of Run It's Chester and Poncho lying in wait on the outside, was quite claustrophobic.

Our intentions were to remove the old hay from every roost and then scrub each roost with lye soap and water. The first nest we began to clean was at the far end of the house. Halfway into removing the dirty hay, we began to gasp for air. It was stifling! The smell from the hay, decorated by urine full of ammonia and chicken poo compounded with the heat, was ghastly. We had created an enormous dust bowl and a powerful stench.

We continued to scoop the old hay out of the roosts until the walkway was full of slimy blobs of green and black chicken poo. Chunks of that mess stuck to our feet like cement and had caked on so hard we needed a sledge hammer and rasp to knock it off.

Tut, deciding to clean his shoes, balanced his body between two of the roosts. He raised his feet at an angle and began to scrape the soles of his shoes against the wall to extract the slimy gunk. Tut scraped so hard that one of his shoes fell onto the walkway. As he began to lift his body up from the roost, his hand mashed a pile of slick poo. He slid forward and landed on his butt. Chicken poo splattered everywhere. Tut reached over, grabbed his shoe and shoved his foot into a shoe full of mess. Tut was fighting mad! Mad at the chickens, chicken house, Poncho, Run It's Chester and most of all because he was covered from head to toe with poo.

As we neared the end of the roosts, I reached into one of the last three cubicles. The hay was thick so I assumed it would be a piece of cake. Wrong! As I cupped my hands under the hay, I could feel an egg buried beneath the mound in the nest. Being careful not to drop the egg, I lifted the egg and started to place it in a clean roost. Just as I reached over to lay the egg down, a sparrow flew through the partially opened window and whizzed past my head. Without realizing what I was doing, I ducked, and my hand with the egg still intact flew upward, releasing the egg toward the ceiling.

Tut started laughing at the sight of me and the sparrow but soon shut his mouth when the egg, still in flight, hit the rafters, cracked open and dropped the putrid, foul-smelling remains on top of his head. That was some bad egg! It smelled as though it had been in the nest for a hundred years.

Tears began to well up in Tut's eyes and he began to gag. The more he gagged, the worse it got! He placed his hand over his mouth to hold back the ever-present upchuck until he got a whiff of the stench on his hands. He couldn't hold it any longer. Racing toward the door, Tut kicked the door open with his foot and heaved toward Poncho and Run It's Chester.

I don't know who was scared the most, Tut or the drenched duo! Tut sat down on the stoop with an exasperated look on his face. He looked up just in time to find the daring duo bearing down on him in full force. Tut stood up, dripping with the rancid egg, spread his legs apart and screamed, "Git! Don't be a messin' with me. Iffen ya bite me, I'm gonna wring yore bloody skinny goozles, pluck yore feathers and bury ya in the backyard!"

I was hysterical with laughter. Every time I looked at Tut, he was doing the dry heaves. I poured some of the cleaning water on top of his head to rinse off the odor. After he sat there for a few minutes, his stomach settled and he came back in to help me finish cleaning.

While he had been sitting on the stoop, I picked up all the dirty hay. Holding my breath to keep from passing out, I cautiously poked the smelly, rotten stuff through the window. The ammonia was enough to choke a horse. We would haul all of the dirty hay and chicken droppings to the barn and cover it with corn shucks. When the litter had cooled from the ammonia, Pa would put it on the garden. It was great fertilizer.

Tut and I started washing down the roosts. It took a long time getting to this point and we were glad we were on the down swing of this job. Tut would take a sudsy, lye-soaped wet rag and soak down the woodwork. I would follow behind and scrub everything with a hard bristled brush.

My head began to itch and I started scratching. It felt as though my hair was crawling down my back. I looked at Tut and he looked at me. As we were looking at one another, we could see little tiny flecks falling between our faces. They were coming from the rafters. As we looked up, sparrow nests lined throughout the rafters were dropping little bird mites.

Bird mites are little tiny insects that attach themselves to bird feathers. For some reason sparrows seem to be most notorious in hosting the itchy crawly little mittie mites. Seeing all these tiny little mites land in our hair was the straw that broke the camel's back.

I took the bucket of water and with a heave flung the rest of the water toward the bird's nests. That set us in motion. We were like a Key Stone Cop movie, going ninety to nothing fast-forwarded with a remote control.

It took us nearly four hours to get through the hassle with Poncho and Run It's Chester, scraping and washing the roosts, gagging and barfing, slipping and sliding, sweeping and heaving and dodging sparrows.

It took all of ten whole minutes to sweep out the birds' nests filled with mittie mites, give the remaining roosts a lick and a promise with a wet rag, pretend they were clean as a whistle, re-line the roosts with fresh hay and vowed to everything holy that we would never clean that chicken house again!

Like I said, cleaning a chicken house is like a battleground. We were surrounded and outflanked by Poncho and Run It's Chester, took direct hits from chicken poo, pelted by a stinking rotten egg, and bombarded with air maneuvers from bird nests filled with mittie mites.

We surrendered! To the coup! General: Poncho, Master Sergeant: Run It's Chester, and Air Defense: Mittie Mites!

# CHARLIE

"It's Charlie, Pa, it's Charlie!" I hollered to everyone in the house. "He's done come back to visit."
Everyone heard me holler and came running to the front stoop. Charlie looked very well, especially after the ordeal he went through. We were surprised to see him, and everyone ran out to give him a big hug. Pa told Charlie to come on in, to have a sit down and bring everyone up to date about the aftermath of his near death and how life was treating him now.
Well, I guess I better tell you the beginning of this story so you can understand why we were so happy to see him. It begins....
I could never understand why anyone could be so bigoted and short-minded toward fellow human beings or why they had the need to slur or defame a character of his being or have the right to plunder and pillage another soul who wished to live in peaceful surroundings.
Although we lived in the hollers and didn't have access to newspapers on a daily basis, have a radio to hear all the latest news, or a telephone to pick up and call our neighbors, Pa and Grampaw would hear, by word of mouth, all the latest gossip about who did this and who did that. Sometimes the news would be bad, and if you didn't want to be caught up in a bad scandal, you kept what you did and who you helped a major secret. Otherwise, you might be on the receiving end of someone making a night visit, unannounced.
Since Pa and Grampaw didn't care one iota about living the

way an outsider thought they should, they continued to help anyone that was down on their luck and had the support of all the hill folk. I guarantee you one thing.... Hill folk bound together had a unity of force. It might have been because hill folk were always thought of as backward sort of people and without common sense, but let me assure you, hill folk had more common sense in their little fingers and more compassion for their fellow man than anyone could ever hope to have.

Another thing, you just didn't mess with hill folk. If anyone decided to go wandering through property at the stroke of midnight, without having a known signal or knew who lived there, you could bet someone would be picking buckshot out of your butt come daylight.

It all happened one day when Tut and I were poking around Hobo cave. We didn't have permission to go to the cave, but sometimes we did things half thinking about the consequences.

We had been walking along the railroad tracks and we'd place our ear down on the tracks every few minutes to hear and feel the rumble of an approaching train. There weren't too many places to escape from a train, unless you slid down the embankment into underbrush or trees. We sure didn't want to run from a train, because doing so we would squash like flies.

We climbed up the steep hill towards the cave because we were bored with kicking rocks and picking up pieces of junk. We had found the pathway when we spent the night in the cave. You remember about that story, don't you? That's when we met Louie and Gus. They were the two hobo's who were searching to find out who they were and what their purpose in life meant. When we took them home with us, Pa had a long talk with them. I didn't know, at the time, what they talked about, but it must have been important.

Well, we had gotten about halfway up the path when we came across a man, lying face down under some bushes. As we cautiously approached him, thinking we had found another dead body, we could hear faint moans. We were afraid to touch him because we didn't know how badly he was hurt. He lifted his head slightly and we could see that blood covered most of his body. Someone had nearly beaten him to a pulp. His face lacerated beneath his eyes, his mouth swollen. You could barely see his entire face because of the dried blood and dirt ground into his skin.

I told Tut to hurry back to the house and bring Pa and Grampaw and the wagon. I would stay with the man until they got back. Being there alone, with a man seriously hurt and the possibility of someone sneaking up behind my back, was not my idea of fun.

Finally, I could hear Pa, Grampaw and Tut. Pa had driven the wagon down the railroad tracks. That scared the daylights out of me. The wagon and horses might be fodder for the next train, because the only way off the tracks was to either manually lift the wagon wheels over the rails and turn the wagon around or continue to drive the team further down the tracks in hopes of finding level ground. Either way, I was fearfully anxious of impending doom. In my mind, all I could see was horses, wagon and train colliding and veering down the embankment. Trains don't stop for anything.

Pa and Grampaw jumped down from the wagon and hurried up the hill. Grampaw lifted the man by his chest while Pa grabbed his legs. They didn't even take time to turn him over or ask him his name.

Going down the hill was a bit tricky. It was hard enough for a single person to descend the hill because of loose gravel sliding under the feet, but to carry another person while their body is face down was a bit precarious.

Tut and I watched Pa and Grampaw as they gently laid the man on the tail of the wagon. Pa leaped into the wagon and pulled the man further up toward the wagon seat. Grampaw, Tut and I jumped up on the wagon bed and Pa drove the wagon nearly a mile down the tracks in order to turn around.

The wagon bounced and banged against the wooden ties holding the rails to the ground. Because the wagon was wider than the rails, the right side of the wagon angled toward the ground in a very awkward slope. If it hadn't been for the horses pulling the wagon forward, the wagon would have surely fallen sideways.

When we neared the clearing, we got off the wagon and raised each of the wagon wheels over the rails. We waited for Pa to turn the wagon around. Then when Pa got the horses in line with the tracks, we lifted the wheels on the right side of the wagon, hopped aboard and headed back down the tracks toward home. Since there was no road close to the tracks, Pa veered off the right side of the rails and headed toward an open field. From there, Pa created a road until we reached the lane near our house. Then Pa opened the reins and the horses headed at full speed.

When we got to the front stoop, Ma was waiting to hold the door open for Pa and Grampaw. Once inside the house, they laid the man on the front bed and began to clean the gaping wounds across his cheeks. It was not until then that we realized the man was of colored skin.

It wouldn't have mattered if the man were green or purple. Pa or Grampaw never judged a man by his color. The only thing that mattered was that a low-down scoundrel had beaten him and left him for dead. He was in dire need of medical help and needed nourishment to help him survive.

Grammaw ladled a big bowl of broth and carried it to the bedside. She sat down on the bed and cradled his head in her lap. Gently speaking to him and placing one half spoonful of broth against his swollen lips, she encouraged him to try to sip more of the broth. The heat of the broth must have been horribly discouraging as I am sure it created pain upon entering his mouth. He took about half of the broth and then, as though

*WINDY JOHN'S RAINBOW AND THE POT O' GOLD*

he knew he was safe from harm, laid his head down and went to sleep.

While he was sleeping, Pa disrobed him, cleaned the gashes on his legs and arms and gently rolled him over on his side. His back looked as though someone had kicked him with steel boots. Very large bruises and whelps were all across his shoulder blades and down around his waist. After Pa had cleaned all the wounds and dressed them with clean cloths, he covered his body with nice warm bedclothes, drew the curtain around the bed and let him sleep. Pa left some of his own clean clothes at the foot of the bed. The man would understand, when he awoke, that it would be necessary to put them on.

Pa gathered up all the old clothes the man was wearing, took them to the cooking hole in the backyard and burned them. If someone came looking for this man, giving a description of those clothes, they wouldn't find him. In fact, Pa would make sure that no one found him to inflict that kind of abuse again.

Grampaw, seeing everything was under control, set off on horseback to see all the hill folk. He wanted to make sure that if anyone came around asking questions, all the answers would be the same. Everyone in the hills understood, in more ways than one, how they felt with someone chastising them verbally and knew the pain it caused for the family. They would do and say whatever Grampaw wanted them to say. Grampaw told them to tell anyone asking to search the perimeters to go ahead. Then, after the people stopped searching, to blow a signal on a cow horn to let the other hill folk know what to expect. If need be, the man would have to be transferred fast from one neighbor to another. That way, the people who tried to inflict the death sentence wouldn't be able to do it again.

The next day, when the man woke up, he was frightened. The last thing he remembered was being on the freight train at night, sitting in a dark corner. Three men approached him, called him degrading names and started to beat him to death.

They said he had no business riding the train and didn't need to be stinking up the air. After one of them hit him in the mouth and sliced his cheek with a knife, the other two began kicking him in the back and then all three men shoved him through the boxcar door. He hit the rocky ground with a thud. He wasn't sure how he crawled up the hill near the cave or that anyone had even rescued him. He didn't even remember having the hot broth touch his lips. He thought he had died when he woke up in the nice warm bed!

Pa looked at him and said, "Son, whut is yore name? I took a telegram frum yore pocket afore I burnt yore wearin' clothes and I knoe why ya had the need to be travlin' the train but ya had nary a cent in yer pockets."

He lowered his head and said, "Suh, my name is Charlie. I be a needin' to git to my momma in south Arkansas. I wus in St. Louie werkin' when the telegram come acros't the wire. My momma's nabor, whut put the notion in my haid to go to St. Louie and checks on my ma, done sent me the telegram. My momma is poorly sick. I be a fearin', Suh, she mite die afore I can git thar. I been a sendin' money fer her to live on. Thet's why I ain't got no money. It takes all my pay jist fer a room, havin' a bite to eat, and helpin' my momma. I'm sorry, Suh, to be a burden. I reckon I best try to git the next train. Iffin I don't, Suh, ya mite be in danger, seeins how them men mite come back. Some men jist don't cotton to my color and shore don't fancy to anyone helpin' me. Suh, ya been kindly but I best be goin'. No Suh, I shore don't want ya to come to any harm!"

Pa, trying to easy the trouble in Charlie's heart, said, "Ya ain't hoppin' thet train. Me and Grampaw will see to gittin' ya to town. Ya wait rite here, me and Grampaw will git the wagon. J.D., fetch old Joe. Tut, you git Sam. Both of ya ride to the Newleys and Joneses. Tell'em to hitch up thar wagons and meet us at the general store. Jist tell'em we gotta git to town. Thay'll knoe whut I mean."

While Pa and Grampaw went to the barn to get the wagon, Tut and I saddled the horses and rode to the neighbors. It didn't take them long to gather up their shotguns, throw some things in the back of the wagon and head toward the general store.

As Tut and I started down the lane to our house, we met Pa and Grampaw. Charlie was hiding under loose hay. Pa told Tut and I to get back home and brush down the horses. We were to keep an eye on the home place. "Keep a watchful eye fer strange men, too. Iffen ya need be, git the spare shotgun hidden in the root cellar. Should thay be any problems, ya knoe whut to do! Yer Grampaw and me should be back frum town afore dark. Don't ferget thar's safety in numbers. Thet's why we got three wagons headed fer town. We'll be jist fine. Git on home now and take care of the wimmin' folk." We watched them as they cleared the lane and headed toward the general store. I hoped and prayed they would be ok.

We had no idea what Pa and Grampaw had planned or who they were going to see in town. I guess it didn't make any difference, cause we all knew when Pa had a plan, things worked out.

This day Tut and I didn't have a devilish scheme in mind. All we figured to do was exactly what Pa and Grampaw said to do. Although we were just youngins, this was serious business and not a time to be having fun. Besides, it felt good to know that Pa and Grampaw trusted us to do the right thing and was secure in leaving us in charge of the home place.

Ma and Grammaw were tougher than cowhide when it came to protecting their youngins, but they realized the importance for me and Tut to have the opportunity to prove our newfound status of being the "men" of the house. Grammaw, Ma and the girls let us have our day in the sun and went along with everything we said. It really felt good for a change, to know we could play the role of protector. Everything went as normal as clockwork. No strange men showed up and we didn't have to shoot anyone in the butt. Probably for the best. Thinking about it now, I'm glad we didn't have to shoot anyone.

Mid afternoon, Pa and Grampaw came home. Charlie was not with them. We were all curious about what happened to Charlie and if they had any kind of trouble. After Pa and Grampaw got their breath of wind and had a bite to eat, we all sat down at the table and listened intently to every word.

When they got to town, Pa said they all pulled their wagons together near the railroad station and casually walked over to the fruit market, bought a few apples and then drove the wagons on down the street. Stopping at the hardware store, Grampaw went inside, bought a pitchfork, came out and rammed it in the hay.

Several burly men had been watching what they were doing and approached Pa to question him, "Whar ya goin' with thet hay? Ya reckon to sell it?"

Grampaw replied to the men, "Done been solt. Gotta git these here loaded down wagons to the bottoms. Thay's a man whut's expectin' us. We best mosey on down the street cause we got a fer piece to go afore we can unload it. Y'all have a good day."

Pa said they went down the street toward the river and turned toward the bottoms. Watching to see if anyone was looking, they cautiously pulled the wagons inside a large open warehouse door. Once inside, the man who would help Charlie greeted Pa, Grampaw and the other two men who aided Charlie's plight.

"Louie, I'm here to collect the faver whut ya said was due me," Pa said as he patted the man's back and shook his hand. Pa began to tell him exactly what he needed and why the urgency. No one should know a thing about what their plan was. Pa pulled back the hay and told Charlie to come with him. Charlie stepped from the wagon and shyly approached this very neatly dressed man. Then they all went in a windowless room.

When they came out of the room, Charlie stayed behind. Then the wagons were unloaded and they drove away.

We thought the story had ended right there until Pa said, "Well, ain't ya gonna ask me whut happened next?"

We all looked at one another and said in unison, "Whut, Pa? Whut happened next. Whar's Charlie?"

"Thought ya would never ask. Do ya member meetin' Gus and Louie in the cave? Well, Louie wasn't an ordinary hobo. He was jist travlin' round to see whut it was like to be without a home and how lots of people lived. Tarned out thet he was a rite nice man who had a real big business. He weren't poor and down on his luck and didn't even have a wife and kid. He jist said all them thangs to see iffen people would tarn up thar noses at him."

"Ya mean our Mr. Louie? The Mr. Louie whut was crien so hard 'bout the little girl whut looked like Effie Mae! Er ya shore, Pa? Well, Pa, thet picture shore nuff looked like Effie Mae. You seed thet picture, Pa! Whar'd he git a picture thet was the spittin' image of Effie Mae?"

"Yup! Jist hold yer horses. Iffen I can git a word in edgewise, I'll tell ya whut I knoe. The day he and Gus hopped the freight, he told me thet iffen I ever needed a faver, to look him up. I nary knoed whar to look. Whilst we were in town a couple of months ago, Mr. Louie came up behind me and tapped me on the shoulder. I shore nuff didn't recognize'em. Thet's when he commenced to tell me 'bout how he appreciated the kind words and vittles and you youngins showin' the love to a stranger. I knoed Mr. Louie would be the man to help Charlie. I knoe yore churnin' in yore britches to find out about thet picture! Mr. Louie told me thet he found the picture whist he was in Kansas. Thar had been a powerful cyclone thet had torn through the plains and had blown the picture near the railroad tracks. He seed the picture, reached down and picked it up. Mr. Louie was as surprised as you youngins were when the picture came alive by seein' Effie Mae. Thet little girl mite be yore cuzzin, frum yer Ma's sister. Mr. Louie told me thet iffen we wanted to find out, he'd shore nuff do whut he could to git us some answers."

Grampaw chimed in, "Mr. Louie is gonna drive Charlie to see his momma. Why, thet man has enough money to burn and don't put up with nobody tellin' him whut to do. In fact, Mr. Louie's gonna give Charlie a job werkin' in the saw mill."

Pa knew that Charlie would be just fine because of what Mr. Louie said, "Yore youngins treated me like family. It didn't matter if I was dirty or I had holes in my clothes. They talked to me when they thought I was hurting and even told me I could live with them, even though they didn't know me. They practically dragged Gus and me home from the cave and insisted that we meet their pa and ma. How we needed to have a family full of love. Those four youngins showed me the purity of helping other people and I made a solemn vow to repay their kindness in words and in deeds."

Pa and Grampaw looked at us with great pride in having repeated what Mr. Louie had told them about us kids.

Now you know the beginning of the story. Charlie was all right! He was sitting in our house and telling us about the outcome of his experience. Mr. Louie did drive him all the way to south Arkansas and stayed with him every minute.

His momma, God rest her soul, did die, but he was there to tell her how much he loved her and was able to thank her for everything she did for him. Mr. Louie paid for Charlie's momma's funeral and later took him to a doctor. Mr. Louie even kept his word about giving Charlie a job.

Charlie was back to tell he would never forget the kindness shown to him in his great time of need. Mr. Louie told him to tell us that, "If we never needed anything, he'd be there. You were there for me and you were there for Charlie. I'll be there for you!"

I thought, *love and compassion knows no color and shouldn't have any bounds holding it back.* Charlie would be just fine and maybe just maybe, we might find out who the little girl was in the picture.

# FOR NOW, R.I.P.

One morning when I was feeling poorly with a sore throat and felt like the whole world was sitting on my neck pushing their elbows through my goozle, Ma made me stay in the house away from everyone. I felt like I was being punished, but I knew it was only to keep everyone from coming down with the same thing. We weren't sick very often, but as nature would have it, occasionally one of us would get the lum-puck-a-roo in our left toenail and feel like our insides were being squeezed through a sieve. My whole body ached and my ears stuck straight out and were blood red.

Indications from my facial expressions made Ma know I was actually sick and not pretending. When my ears turned red Ma knew I had fever. We didn't have a fever thermometer and really didn't need one. Ma knew in an instant, by placing her cheek against our foreheads, whether our body temperature was waging war against some foreign germ. Not only that ... our eyeballs sank back inside our skulls, making us look like powdered-up zombies, and we walked like limp dishrags.

When we turned down food, Ma knew to pile extra quilts on top of us. The fever needed to be broken, and quilts on top of quilts, tucked under the feet tighter than a tied up corset, plastered the body in one position with no possible way of turning over, making the whole body sweat like a raging river. I was never sure if all that sweat was from fever or of not being able to move or finding some way out from under the ton of quilts when the bodily functioning urge was necessary.

As I lay there, I thought about the awful-tasting medicine Ma poked down my throat. It tasted like someone had ground up bitter old horehound candy and mixed it with creosote with a pint of white lightning or turpentine for good measure. It would burn the hairs right out of your nose and curl up your toenails, not to mention burn the hell out of your throat. It burned going in and coming out!

Then I remembered Old Doc Herb and why Grammaw knew how to concoct those awful mustard plasters for chest congestion and the elixir from hell. There was no doctor close at hand, except for the "doctor of herbs" that lived in the holler. He wasn't an actual doctor with a degree but had lived for so long that he knew just about every homemade remedy ever concocted. Although everyone knew he was partially blind, it didn't stop persons from asking what home remedy they should use for an earache to arthritis.

You could see Old Doc Herb gathering various sorts of wild grasses, flower petals and bark of pine trees. He would stoop to smell the flowers before picking, run his hand over the blades of grass to make certain he had the right variety and pound tree trunks to release faint odors for certain concoctions. He always knew when each herb was ready to pick. Placing each little petal into the center of his straw hat, he would make his way back to his kitchen to prepare medicine for anyone needing his assistance.

He was a frail-looking, gentle person, stoop-shouldered with a little round paunch of stomach protruding as though he hadn't eaten for awhile. The waist of his trousers, held up by suspenders, came nearly up to his chest, making the pant legs higher than the tops of his socks. It appeared that he was treading water as he shuffled about on his front porch. In fact, he was probably healthier than most people could ever imagine and didn't care about his appearance.

When I drifted back from the thoughts of Old Doc Herb, I

realized this had to be one of the most boring days I ever encountered. While I was cooped up in the loft sweating my brains out, feeling as if a porcupine had invaded my skin, Tut and the girls were having a grand old time in the front yard. I secretly wished they were as sick as a goat and at the same time hoped they didn't catch what I had.

Ma would check on me every few minutes and bring a soothing wet rag to wipe my brow. It had to be hard on Ma, cause I was stuck in the loft and she was the one climbing up and down the ladder. Being a kid, I didn't think much about climbing the ladder, but for Ma and Grammaw, it had to be rough on the knee joints. After the umpteenth time with Ma scaling the ladder, I asked her to bring me a jug full of water to drink and I would wipe my own brow with cool water when I felt like it.

While I was lying there, bored out of my mind, I picked up the grayish old rag that I had been using to wipe off the sweating fever and held it up in the air. It was about one foot square with neatly sewn edges. The thread holding it together was coming loose at one end and I pulled on the thread, wrapping it tightly around my finger. The rag bunched up with tiny little gathers making a mini parachute as all the ends met together in the center. Trying to undo what I did broke the thread and I wound up with the tip of my finger blood red, encased with skin gouging thread pulsating with the beat of my heart. I had cut the circulation off to my finger and the old rag was turning into an unraveled mess. I had killed the rag and nearly cut off my finger!

As I was deciding how to explain the death of the old rag to Ma, I wadded it up into a ball and hid it under the quilts. My brain was going ninety to nothing when I decided to make some kind of puppet out of the rag to keep me occupied.

I took all four corners together, twisted it into a rope and tried to turn it inside out. It still looked like a stupid, wadded-up rag. In desperation, I began rolling it into a long, cigar-shaped snake. Then I tied one end into a knot, unrolled the loose end and folded the material over the knot. Staring at the puppet, it began to take shape. All I needed was one of Ma's needles to stitch the little critter into the image which was unfolding right before my eyes.

As I sneaked down from the loft, being very careful not do draw suspicion upon myself, I took a needle and some white tatting thread from Ma's sewing case and climbed back into the loft. The loosened thread, which had nearly cut off my finger, was the tie to bind all the ends together. Squinting to poke the thread through the eye of the needle, in my haste to get the job done, I dropped the needle among the quilts. The old saying, "A needle in a haystack is hard to find" is pure rot! I found it as I sat down. It rammed in my thigh and I let out a yell that reverberated against the loft ceiling.

Ma ran to the ladder and asked me what was wrong. I told her that I bit my tongue. It wasn't a lie! I actually did bite my tongue when I sat down on the needle, but I just didn't tell her the whole truth as to why my tongue was hanging out of my mouth in the first place.

Everyone, at one time or another, engrossed in doing a project, has unfortunately placed their tongue between their teeth for a better grip. I will tell you one danged thing! That was the last time my tongue aided me in any project. So far, I was sick as a goat, I nearly chopped my finger off, my tongue swelled bigger than a goose egg and my thigh was throbbing from a needle puncture.

After a few minutes of coaxing the thread into the eye of the needle, I began stitching my "partner." Within a few minutes, there he sat with his long tail, whiskers and eyes and had a very long string attached to his back. It was the spitting image of a long-tailed, big-bellied gray rat. Up to this point, I hadn't felt like being rotten but after staring at Raggie the Rat, a mischievous scheme began to form in my mind.

Before I could lay my plan in motion, Ma and Grammaw dashed to the front yard. Baby Jo was squalling her eyes out and Tut, Effie Mae and Aunt Sukie was complaining that they didn't feel good. One by one, they came inside the kitchen moaning and groaning. I knew exactly how they felt and was sorry I secretly hoped they would be sick too.

Ma and Grammaw were being run ragged. Baby Jo didn't want to lie down cause her "fwoat" hurt and the rest of them were complaining of itching all over their bodies. Baby Jo was in Grammaw's room and Effie Mae and Aunt Sukie were hunkered in the front room. Tut was on a pallet near the kitchen and I was in the loft. After a little persuasion and pleading with Ma, Tut joined me in the loft. If we were all going to be sick, we might as well be sick together.

Tut climbed the ladder and plopped down on the mattress. He was hotter than a red-hot poker and looked worse than what I expected. As he began to pull the quilts up around his neck, Raggie the Rat fell out of the rafters where I had placed him for safekeeping and landed smack dab on Tut's face. Now, Tut was sick, but it sure didn't keep him from moving on the opposite side of me as he yelled, "Thar's a da-da-da-danged rat. Take sumthin' and wh-wh-wh-whack it!" He was freaking out in the loft and wasn't doing my headache a favor. When he realized the rat was only an old dishrag, he was relieved and knew it wouldn't be long before Ma or Grammaw would be on the receiving end of the rat. He just looked at me and smacked me on the head, put his head down and went to sleep. At that point, I realized how tired I was and closed my eyes.

I'm not sure how long I had been asleep, but the nap made me feel much better and I was ready to extract myself from the loft. As I stood up to climb down the ladder, Raggie the Rat had somehow been pushed to the edge of the loft and the string attached to his back was wound around one of the railings.

Before I knew what was happening, Grammaw let out a high-pitched wail, grabbed up the old straw broom and came down with the force of a hammer beating the floor to death. Somehow, the force of the broom flung Raggie the Rag into the loft while Grammaw was continuing her search of the floor hunting for the ugly old rat. I was just about down the ladder when Grammaw grappled me by the nape of the neck, jerked me from the ladder and proceeded to scale the loft: with the broom secured tightly in her hand.

When she got into the loft, Tut, barely awake from his stupor, saw Grammaw standing there stooped-shouldered with the broom above her head, her eyes wilder than a peach orchard boar and thought that he was about to meet his maker. Quilts and pillows went flying through the air with tremendous force, the jug of water upended and soaked Tut and the quilts. Tut was out of his mind seeing Grammaw pound the loft in a wild rage and woke up in one fine hurry.

Raggie the Rat swept out of the loft and gingerly landed at my feet. Now I realized why Grammaw was rampant and why Tut thought a ghoulish nightmare had captured him.

By now, everyone rattled awake was standing at the foot of the loft watching Grammaw do the Saint Vitus' dance in the loft. Ma, having been out gathering eggs, came running to see why Grammaw was in such a frenzy and stumbled over the mound of quilts. We kids watched as the basket of eggs she was carrying went flying through the air like modern-day frisbees and standing there cemented motionless to the floor, waited patiently as one by one, the eggs came crashing down on our heads. We stood there looking like omelets with egg yolks dripping down our faces as Grammaw peeked over the railing with a sheepish grin on her face. Ma was sprawled across the quilts in a dazed shock.

"Didja see thet thang scamperin' acrost the floor?"

"Whut thang? I ain't seein' anythang but speckled kids!"

"Thar's a durn big old ugly rat somewhar in the house! We best be a findin' it afore it chews through the floor. We cain't be a havin' it make babies. Jist as soon as we git the kids warshed up frum the egg goop, we best be huntin' it."

I knew I had better keep my mouth shut or they were going to sweep Raggie the Rat and me into the front yard or make mince meat out of my hide. As I very carefully placed Raggie the Rat in my pocket, I looked at Tut. There was something mighty peculiar about his face and it wasn't egg yolk! In fact, Effie Mae, Aunt Sukie and Baby Jo looked the same way. It was as though someone had been finger painting with red rocks that we called Indian paint and splattered it across their cheeks. Before I could say a word, Ma caught a glimpse of my face and said, "J.D. whar have ya been? Have ya been in the nettles agin'? Yore face is redder than a beet."

"Ma, I ain't been in the nettles. I'm a itchin' but ya know I ain't been outside today."

As Ma inspected my face, she said, "Grammaw, ya best be a checkin' the rest of them. I suspect they done come down with the measles. If it ain't one thang, it's another. We got egg goo everwhar, the quilts'er soakin' wet, we done got rats runnin' through the house and the kids'er itchin'! Whut's next?"

Ma barely got through asking that question when Pa and Grampaw came sauntering through the front door. Seeing all the havoc, they wanted to know what in thunder had happened and why all of us looked like scrambled eggs in beet juice. Ma said very snappily, "Git outta here. We got us a powerful mess to clean up. The kids'er itchy, rats'er in the house and me and Grammaw ain't in no mood fer the likes of you two. Ya best be a tippy toeing right back out the door."

"Hell's bells," Grampaw said, "I'm headin' fer the barn. If ya know whut's good fer ya, Pa, ya best be a followin' me in my footsteps. It looks like a battlefield in here and I ain't got the notion to be on the receivin' end of the cannon balls! We'll come back when the smoke clears, iffen it ever does." Both of them stayed in the barn or out in the yard for the better part of the day.

After Ma hung the quilts out to dry, she cleaned the egg goop from our itchy bodies and the floor. Grammaw rubbed a baking soda paste on our bodies to keep the itching to a minimum. Our faces looked like funny red speckled ghosts. With a little bit of flour, some more eggs and a little bit of sugar mixed with all the baking soda, I am sure we all could have arisen to ghostly heights.

When the girls turned their backs from Tut and me, I slowly pulled Raggie the Rat from my pocket. Tut, peering through the baking soda, gasped when he realized Grammaw was hunting a nonexistent critter. "Whut ya goin' to do with thet thang, J.D.? Iffen Grammaw finds out she was killin' the floor for nuthin', ya might be the next critter she gits after. Ya got thet look on yer face. Whut ya got up yore sleeve?"

"Well, I been a figgerin' to poke it in the kitchen. Ya know thet old flour can sittin' by the cookstove? Well, I figger thet thay'll be usin' the flour fer biskits and when thay poke thar hands down inside the can to scoop up the flour, thay'll find the old ugly rat thay was chasin'."

"Grammaw's goin' to kill you, J.D. Thay're goin' to be a plantin' yore rotten butt in the backyard along with thet rat. How ya reckon ta pull it off? Hey, I know, I'll yell real loud, thay'll both come runnin' and whilst thay do, ya mosey inta the kitchen sayin' ya need some drinkin' water. Thet outta give ya time to stick it inta the flour tin."

It sounded like a foolproof scheme. Tut did his little screaming fit, and on cue, Ma and Grammaw went running. I went into the kitchen and was just about to cram old Raggie the Rat inside the flour tin when Pa and Grampaw came through the back door. I hid Raggie the Rat up under my armpit and decided to wait on another day to scare Ma and Grammaw. Unfortunately, I didn't have another opportunity to follow through with the scheme and decided to put Raggie the Rat away for safekeeping. It would just have to wait.

That evening, after a day full of sweats, sore throats, hair stripping creosote elixir, rats, eggs and being itchy, all us kids went to bed. To tell you the truth, we were exhausted! We wanted to crawl into bed and didn't put up a howl about anything, even a double dose of the elixir from hell. Every one of us must have slept very soundly, because we didn't even hear the stack of firewood fall and roll from the back porch.

The next morning when Grammaw approached the backdoor to retrieve kindling, she noticed someone had not shut the door properly. It was partially ajar. She knew the old door sometimes would swell from damp night air and didn't pay any attention or care that it was open. Grampaw probably left it ajar making his early morning trek to the outhouse.

As I lay in the loft, just slightly awake and feeling much better than the day before, I was anxious to resume a somewhat normal routine. Nothing could remotely top the previous day's activity. Or so I thought! Pretty soon the whole house was awakened with thunderous sounds of pots and pans clanking together, kindling wood being thrown against the old kitchen table, a sifting tin soared through the air and white flour residue began covering the entire house.

Grammaw was spewing forth a string of depletives as a four-legged critter scampered over kindling trying to get away from Grammaw's deadly aim.

Straight into the bedroom it ran, leaving footprints in the sifted flour trying to get a firm foothold in making the great escape. Grammaw was hot on his heels. As she entered the bedroom, Grampaw raised his head from the pillow, only to find Grammaw covered from head to toe in flour, her long hair sticking out in all directions, a piece of kindling wood in one hand and a butcher knife in the other.

"Didja see it? Whar'ed it go?"

"Woman, ya scairt the hell outta me. Don't be a standin' over me lookin' like thet and stop a wavin' thet butcher knife. Whut ran up yore drawers?"

"It was thet damned old rat. It poked its haid outta the flour tin and lunged fer me. I'm nigh on to cuttin' out its goozle!"

"Iffen ya don't stop wavin' thet butcher knife yore liable to cut off yore own cock-eyed haid. Git a grip, Grammaw, git a grip!"

As Grampaw placed his feet on the floor, the biggest and ugliest, old gray wire-haired, long-tailed, razor-sharp-toothed opossum ran hissing out from under the bed. It went between Grampaw's feet and around Grammaw faster than you could snap your fingers.

This opossum was scared to death because he just met up with something bent out of shape and wilder than a wart hog and probably knew if he pretended to be asleep or dead, he would wind up as soup stock. The backdoor didn't have a chance to shut because the opossum, in its endeavor to stay alive, slid through sifted four with his toenails clawing the floor, shot over pots and pans and went through that door like greased lightning. His only safety was in the underbrush or in the treetops. At least there, he would have chance to thwart death without coming in contact with a machete-wielding lunatic.

None of us kids dared to get out of bed until Grammaw calmed down. Tut poked me in the ribs and whispered, "J.D. whar did ya poke thet old rat. Grammaw's goin' to be nuts all day iffen she finds thet critter hidden whar it shouldn't be."

"Tut, I done figgered the same thang! It ain't full sunup yet, but my brain's done been revealed the light. I ain't hangerin' to be on the receivin' end of Grammaw's wrath. Come full light, Raggie the Rat will find his true restin' place."

Grammaw calmed down after she cleaned up the mess and then the adults went out on the front porch. I could hear them laughing about the wild things happening and I felt relieved. Laughter was the best medicine for what ailed a person and we all were feeling better. Being sick wasn't so bad, especially when all the laughter made the soul and spirit lift to great heights from the unexpected, early morning visitor.

Walking in the kitchen, I cautiously and quietly lifted the trapdoor leading down into the root cellar and made my way through the darkened, cold storage room and lovingly placed Raggie the Rat upon a ledge behind some of Ma and Grammaw's canned goods. He would be safe from any butcher knife and close at hand if I ever needed his assistance again.

For the time being, I was off the hook from causing the ruckus and delighted that my dead rag critter, better known as Raggie the Rat, turned into a real live, wild-eyed, scared to death, get-me-the-hell-out-of-here, four-legged critter that just happened to wander into the right place at the wrong time.

Here's to you, Raggie the Rat, and for now, R.I.P.

# HORACE

Ma used to say, "Ya better mind whut ya say and be on the watch fer angels. Ya jist never know when ya might be entertainin' an angel or when one will be knockin' on the door. Cain't rightly say whut thay look like but iffen the Bible says thay exist, in Hebrews 13:2, well, ya best not take nuthin' fer granted." As a kid, I remember whatever Ma and Pa said always rang truth. I might not have understood the profound nature of their wisdom, but I cautiously employed my brain to be on the lookout for angels.

In my own way of thinking, I could visualize angels dancing in a grand and glorious array of puffy angelhair clouds. Angels surely must have been the most wonderful adaptations of human figures, standing guard over a wayward soul or one in need of assistance. The picture in my mind of how angels should look appeared almost without question. Larger than life they would be, with powerful, compassionate arms wide enough to embrace the world. Gently flowing hair of golden blonde, draped down to the knees, shined and glimmered through rays of sunlight reflected by God's own vision.

Wide massive wings, whiter than snow and softer than cotton, swirled their loveliness to lofty places and directed their love and attention to those in need. The attire of an angel could only have been white silk, draping and folding the purity of perfection. Angels could walk on water and nothing could stop the love flowing from their hearts.

I suppose the picture of angels in my mind might have been

directly related to a picture Pa purchased in town. The angel in the picture was most lovely and exuded a tender, warm glow around the face with a halo brighter than gold. I secretly wished I could reach out and touch an angel or turn around and see one standing behind me.

Enter Horace. Horace and his family had lived in the holler for about one year. Horace was an only child and didn't seem to have a care in the world, even though on occasion, a grimace would rock his face and jolt his senses to the point of rigidity.

The reason Horace and his family moved to the holler is partly because of Pa. While in town one day, Pa had noticed a young boy standing near an old lamppost. His face had turned white as a sheet and he was gasping for a breath of fresh air. Usually the air in town reeked with animal droppings or someone revving up the smoky engine on an old automobile. Pa scooped him up in his arms and ran inside the general store, yelling for help. Before Pa could snap his fingers, several people were there. They were eager to help Pa and Horace. Luckily for Pa, the young boy's parents saw what had happened and rushed over to take charge. That's when Pa became friends with the Landskis.

Apparently, the Landskis had been traveling for some time trying to find a suitable place to raise their son, Horace, who was not in the best of health. They told Pa about Horace being a sickly little child since birth and traveling for so long had taken its toll on all of them. They were tired, hungry and, most of all, desperate for somewhere to call their own. They weren't asking for any handouts. All they needed was a sympathetic ear.

Pa, being the kind of person who couldn't stand seeing anyone in desperation, told the Landskis he knew a place they could live if they wanted to live in the country. Pa told them he had to do some business in town and when he returned to the general store, if they were still interested, they could follow him to the "hollers." Pa was gone for about one hour and sure enough, when he returned to the general store; they were waiting for him, eager to have a new life, in a new home, and around new friends.

The new home for the Landskis was over the ridge behind Mr. Matlock's general store. It wasn't the perfect place, but at least the roof didn't leak. There was a fireplace, and most of all, with a little work the old, abandoned house could become a home. It took a little while to make it livable, but after wiping the cobwebs from the rafters, nailing loose floorboards down and putting all their furniture in place, the old house took on a personality of its own.

I will never forget the first time I met Horace nor the events leading up to our initial contact. Rain was pouring down from the heavens and the sky didn't appear to mind one little bit. The clouds were exuberant as they emitted the large raindrops; watching as each drop pelted the ground to create puddles of muddy water. It had been unusually dry and the smell of rain hitting the dusty old lane and calming blades of grass that beckoned for moisture was truly a welcome sight. Since the rain forced all of us into the house, any chores would have to wait. That in itself was rewarding but boring, to say the least.

Pa, sensing my boredom, asked if I would like to take a hike. It would be fun to stomp through the mud holes and smell the new clean air. I tried to persuade Tut to come along, but he wasn't too anxious to go traipsing out into the elements. Pa and I bundled up and headed out the front door.

"Whar we goin', Pa?"

"I figure we'd go ta the general store and maybe grab up a hunk'a them pickles. I done got a hangerin' flung on me fer pickles. Why, we might even find us a stick'a chewin' gum. Don't rightly know iffen pickles and gum taste good together, but we'll soon find out!"

I loved being with Pa. He made the dreariest old day turn

into sunshine and made me smile. Especially talking about those pickles!

As we walked through the rain, getting drenched to the bone, I felt the urge to hug Pa. Even though I knew the rain was cool against the skin; somehow the rain felt warm. Pa gingerly took his big old arm and draped it around my shoulders, and we laughed as each foot kerplopped in squishy friendly mud holes. Pa was much older than me but young at heart and never missed an opportunity to enjoy the simple pleasures of life. I suppose he knew what I needed before I did!

As we approached the general store, I could smell the smoky hickory aroma of burning logs releasing from the black pot-bellied stove inside the general store. We wiped our muddied feet and tried to shake the water off our clothes before we entered the store.

The old wooden door creaked through rusty old iron hinges as we lifted the latch and walked inside. As our eyes adjusted to the dimly lit store, we could see Mr. Matlock standing near the stove, his backside almost glowing with the heat that exuded from the warmth of the hickory embers.

His old meerschaum pipe, dangling from his lips, was releasing a faint aroma of cherry tobacco, and each exhaled puff of tobacco smoke curled around his head in perfect smoke rings. The aura of the general store etched perfectly in my mind. I could never forget the happiness I was feeling.

We stayed at the general store for quite sometime. While the two of them talked, I explored every nook and cranny; lifting the old glass lids on the candy jars, perusing an old book with pictures, rearranging canned goods on the rickety old shelves and smelling the brine of the pickle keg. It was an adventure of old but new things. Mr. Matlock allowed me to venture into the backside of the store.

Since the store was sandwiched inside a hill, I often wondered what was beyond the back curtain. Today I found the answer! As I pulled back the curtained door that divided the store, it was as though I had stepped through a looking glass. It was the living quarters of Mr. Matlock. However, it was not a normal place to live!

It was a huge cave, made into a house. The walls were laden with boulders and used for shelves. The pot-bellied stove was near the wall of the store; the flue angled through a piece of old tin roofing. There was an old ladder-backed chair and a table adorned with an old coal oil lantern placed near the stove. On one side of the cave was an old iron bed covered with mounds of quilts. Old pictures of a beautiful woman caught my eye and I wondered who she was. Before I could explore further fascinating things, Pa yelled for me to come on.

As I exited the newly found premises, Mr. Matlock smiled real big and said, "Thet big old cave made me feel jist like ya feel right now, J.D. Why, I reckon when I first laid eyes on this here cave, I knowed thet it would be a right good place to call my own. I suppose yore wonderin' who thet woman is, ain't ya? She wus my lovin' wife, but she's been gone now, fer many a yar. Not a day goes by thet I don't think of her or remember the good times we had together. Thet's in the past, though. By the way, J.D., ya ain't seen nuthin' yet! One'a these days, iffen ya bring Tut along, we'll mosey further inside the cave. Thar's a cave beyond my livin' quarters thet has the biggest old rocks hangin' down frum the ceilin' and rocks reachin' up toards the ceilin'. Looks like a giant dragon with thar mouths wide open. It gits mighty cold in thar, too! Ya best be gittin' on with yore Pa. Jist don't ferget!"

Forget! How in thunder was I supposed to forget what Mr. Matlock just told me? I was in such a fog that I didn't realize where Pa was taking me.

Pa was carrying five pickles wrapped up in a clean handkerchief and sticks of chewing gum shoved down in his pocket. I had completely forgotten about our purpose for going to Mr. Matlock's store. Before I knew it, we had reached the top of the hill and were walking toward an old house.

My heart raced as I realized we were standing on the same sod where Rainbow and I had formed our meaningful and wonderful friendship. As I looked toward the front stoop, I could see someone peering from a small window. Pa stepped upon the stoop and knocked on the door.

When the door opened, there stood Horace. He was about nine years old, and his skin was whiter than a sheet. To top it off, his hair was whiter than the sheet and all you could see was blue eyes peering through white eyelashes. If it hadn't been for his blue eyes, a body could have missed seeing him at all. He seemed as frail as a chicken egg and I thought he would surely break if he bent over.

Standing there, giving each other the once-over, I pushed my hand forward to shake his hand. To my surprise, the grip of his hand was more than I expected. It was as though he was telling me not to underestimate his frail body. While we were getting acquainted, Pa and his folks were sitting at the kitchen table, making small talk and drinking coffee.

The rain had stopped and I asked Horace if he would like to go outside. He answered, "I cain't go outside. Iffen I do, I git the deep wheezes." I stood there looking at him wondering, *Just what the heck are deep wheezes.* He laughed and said, "The deep wheezes is when I cain't git my breath and I make the rattlin' sounds."

The look on my face must have been puzzling, because Horace began telling me about the horrible times he could not breathe and would wake up in the middle of the night gasping for air. His lungs would rattle, making funny sounds like there was water inside his lung cavities. "Many times I really wondered iffen I was goin' to die."

Horace asked his momma if he could go outside and stand for a while. He promised his ma that he would not overexert himself and wouldn't stay outside too long. That's when Horace explained that he had never been able to play with other kids because of his breathing difficulties. In fact, the dust around the hollers made his breathing more labored and they were thinking of moving to another part of the country. He didn't know where, just anywhere to keep him alive.

He told me that on occasion he would sneak off to be by himself and think about how everyone's life might be much better if he weren't around. Although he thought crazy things, he knew his momma and poppa loved him very much. He wouldn't hurt his momma and poppa by telling them his deep dark secrets.

I sat there for the longest time listening to Horace, nodding as though I understood what he was saying. He told me that his name was Horace Aaron Landskis. He hated the name Horace, didn't like his middle name and almost couldn't tolerate anyone calling him HAL – his initials. His momma called him Angel when they were by themselves. Not in public! That made everyone think he was a sissy.

After awhile, I began telling him about our family and some of the things that Tut and I had done to be ornery. He laughed so hard that tears streamed down his cheeks and began coughing so hard I thought he would pass out. Then I told him about the cave that Mr. Matlock lived in. His eyes got bigger than saucers and he made me promise to take him along when Tut and I went to explore the cave. I hesitantly said yes but was afraid what would happen if he got too far away from the security of his house.

It was nice talking to Horace. He was a gentle soul with great compassion for everything and loved learning about new and exciting things. His wisdom for such a small boy left a lump in my throat. An hour went by and Pa told me we needed to get on home. As Pa and I walked down the mountainside, he explained the urgency of getting to know Horace and why we went there to visit with them.

Several days later, there was a timid little knock at our door. When I opened the door, there stood Horace. He had sneaked off and wanted to go see the caves. Since I knew how difficult it was for Horace to breathe, I asked Ma to wet a rag and place it across his nose and mouth. He could breathe in moisture to keep his lungs from drying out.

When I told Ma what Horace wanted, she became frantic. Luckily, Pa was in the barn and Tut went there to fetch him. Pa dropped what he was doing and came to the house to take charge of the situation. Pa told us to go on to the store, explore for a few minutes and then get Horace back to his house. With a wet rag wrapped around Horace's face, the three of us set off for the general store.

We were halfway down the lane when we stopped dead in our tracks. Tut said, "Thar's someone yellin'. Thay sound jist like thay're cussin'! Listen. Thar it goes agin'. It shore nuff sounds like thay need thar mouths scrubbed with the lye soap."

Horace stood there, blushing a faint shade of pink. "J.D., ya 'member when I told ya thet I hated my names. Jist listen fer the next yell. I reckon yer gonna find out why!"

We stood there motionless waiting for the next blast of cuss words.

Yup, it was apparent. Hor ... ASS! Hor ... ASS! Ha ... LL! Ha ... LL! It sounded like someone was telling an ass to go to hell.

"Why don't she jist yell, Aaron? It shore nuff would be better than makin' yore ears tarn red."

"Well, I told a fib. Thet ain't my middle name. I ain't telling nary a soul whut my middle name is. I done told Momma iffen she yells my middle name, I ain't never comin' home."

Gathering our senses, we made our way to the general store. Relating the circumstances to Mr. Matlock, he told us to go ahead and check out the first cave but not to venture inside the back cave without him. We looked at every nook and cranny in the cave and found some very interesting objects. It was rather damp in the cave from all the rain, but Horace didn't cough at all. In fact, there was no rattle in his lungs. It was as though he was breathing quite normally and taking very deep, soothing breaths.

Mr. Matlock joined us in the cave and told us to join hands before we went into the back cave. Mr. Matlock lit the coal oil lantern and lifted the old curtain dividing the two caves. When we entered the cave, it was gorgeous. It appeared to have various colors painted over the surface of the cave, and very large, sharp-pointed rocks were reaching for the ceiling. Large formations of rocks were holding on to the ceiling, dripping droplets of water toward the floor. It sounded so peaceful inside the cave.

Occasional drips of water landing into small pools of water made all of us listen to the next inevitable drop of water. The moisture in the cave made the atmosphere very cold, and I was wishing I had on a coat.

Mr. Matlock broke the silence by saying; "This is the place whar I poke the fresh vegetables to keep 'em fresh. Why, it's jist like walkin' inta an icebox, only it ain't got no ice! Now ya know why I never git hot on the summer day. I jist mosey inta the cave and cool off."

I'm not sure how long we were there. I do know that Horace was having the best time and I almost hated having to take him home. As we were walking out the door, we could hear the frantic yell of his mother and saw his poppa walking to the store with a panicked look on his face. When he saw Horace, he reached out and hugged Horace so hard I thought his eyeballs would pop right out of their sockets. He wasn't angry with Horace; only relieved to know that he was okay.

When we explained why we were at the store and that Horace hadn't coughed one time while being in the caves, it made his poppa realize that they needed to be in an area with cool moisture.

Not too long after our adventure, the Landskis moved away from the hollers. I never found out where they went but did find out Horace's middle name.

Do you remember me telling you about Angels and how they sometimes visit without announcing their presence? Well, we were in the presence of an angel; one who made all of us see the glory in being alive and gave us a reason for not taking for granted the joy of seeing a new daybreak forth in every season. Horace didn't like his name but I loved his middle name.... It was ANGEL.

# Epilogue
# THE JOURNEY ENDED

Daddy was tired. Telling the stories as he laughed and cried over the wonderful life he had and seeing the exuberance wane from the sparkle in his eyes, I could tell he was ready to complete his life journey. His once powerful arms and massive body had dwindled into a sweet little old man waiting for "his rewards."

On a Sunday morning in 1995, as I approached his room in the nursing home, I stopped short of entering. The nurse told me he was not responding to anyone and what to expect when I entered the room. As I went closer to his bed, he was in labored breathing. I took his hand in mine and spoke softly in his ear. I told Daddy it was ok, he didn't have to worry about me or my sister, Hazel. We would be fine.

Down the hallway, just inside the lunchroom, a small church service was beginning. A chorus of heavenly music filtered around our ears and into our hearts. A trio of singers was singing a song Daddy loved to sing, "When They Ring Those Golden Bells for You and Me." The words to the song held such promise and were sung with great tenderness. When I told him that Momma and those he loved were waiting on him, he turned his head toward me and smiled. A single tear slipped from his steel blue eyes as they softly closed for the last time. Daddy was at peace.

From all the notes I had taken as Daddy told me these stories and more, I quickly released them from memories to paper. It was such a blessing to know that his stories would never be lost. As I penned each story, I remembered how his eyes would light up, the gusto of his roaring belly laugh, tears trickling down his cheeks from the uncontrollable laughter or reminiscences of long-ago antics and his endless love for telling stories; I knew in my heart this was truly a legacy of love.

Till we meet again.... Bye, bye Daddy.
With love,

Your daughter, Joyce